Catch Your Breath

Kathryn J. Bain

Copyright © 2012 by Kathryn J. Bain

Cover by Nicola Martinez

All rights reserved. No part of this publication may be reproduced, stored in a retrieval system, or transmitted by any means – electronic, mechanical, photographic (photocopying), recording, or otherwise – without prior permission in writing from the author.

This is a work of fiction. As such, any names, characters, places, incidents, and dialog are either the products of the author's imagination or used in a fictitious manner. Any resemblance to actual places, events, or persons (living or dead) is purely coincidental.

To find out more about this book or the author, visit: www.kathrynjbain.com[1]

---

1. http://www.kathrynjbain.com

Dedication

I'd like to thank all my critique group partners who are constantly showing me I'm never finished when I think I am. Thanks to my family for their patience while I fulfill my life's dream.

To receive updates regarding upcoming releases, book signings, sales, sign up for my newsletter at https://landing.mailerlite.com/webforms/landing/g4n8h9.

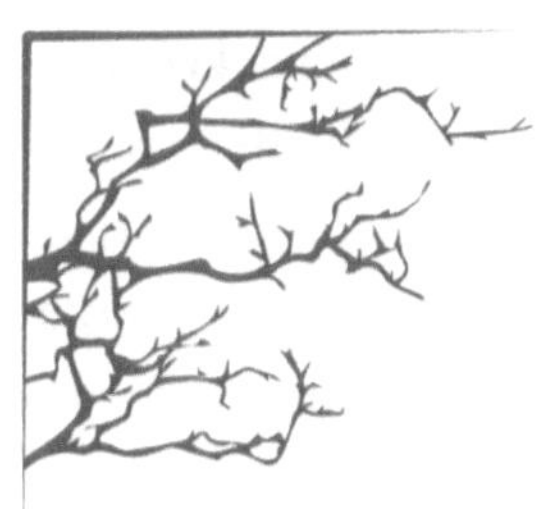

1

The woman leaned against the building across the street from the art shop. She glanced at the store every few seconds. Her jacket was different, but the cap was the same, and so were the suede boots. Calley Regan swore she was the same person she'd seen earlier. Besides, with the temperature in the upper eighties, why wear a jacket unless you were trying to hide?

"You noticed her too?" Her boss, Eva Martinez, placed her coffee mug in the microwave. She walked up and looked over Calley's shoulder. "I spotted her when I got in this morning. You don't think she's planning to rob the place or is a lookout for someone else, do you?"

"Not with those Cesare Paciotti boots." Calley hated anxiety. Why did so many people have to make other's lives miserable?

"Maybe she stole them." Eva's red lipstick almost disappeared with the tightening of her lips.

Her tone cast a hint of fear, which only added to Calley's concern. She wasn't about to let on that she'd seen the same person outside her apartment that morning. Eva was already over-protective. This would only make her worse.

"It doesn't matter what she wants," Eva said. "There's no way she's getting in that door." After a kid high on drugs robbed the store several months ago, she bought a state-of-the-art alarm system, complete with a locked door and buzzer to allow entrance.

Most burglars didn't bother with their small shop. The E. Martinez Gallery of Fine Used Art sold paintings on consignment and not from any world-renowned artists. They kept only a small amount of cash in

1

the drawer. The guy who'd robbed the store months before walked away with a whopping sixteen dollars, ten of which came from Calley's purse.

Calley turned back to the window. Nothing about the woman's appearance stuck out except the five-hundred-dollar boots. Similar Brave's caps were owned by thousands in the area, and the jacket was something you could pick up at any local department store.

The stranger looked up, and her eyes met Calley's. She seemed unfazed that anyone was aware of her presence. Her lack of concern unnerved Calley. The microwave dinged, causing Calley to jump.

"She has an evil stare." Eva walked back to the kitchen area. "You know what they say. The eyes are the window to the soul. Her eyes tells me she's an unhappy lady."

Calley's belly fluttered like small wings of an angel. She patted the growing lump at her midsection. "Don't worry. I'll make sure nothing happens to you. Not even five months and already active. Just like your father." She joined Eva in the back.

"Too bad most of his activity involved screwing around." Eva poured liquid creamer into her instant coffee. The aroma of almonds covered the small kitchen space.

The moment Peter Jameson found out about the baby, he announced he was married and wanted nothing more to do with her or their unborn child. Calley lowered herself into a rolling chair behind her desk a few feet from the small refrigerator. Tears formed at the rim of her eyes. She had to stop this. She'd cried way too much for a man who turned out to be a loser.

"I'm sorry. That was cold of me." Eva pushed her wavy brown hair over her shoulder and walked over to Calley. "You'll be fine. And you'll make a great mom." She took a sip of coffee and sat down on the edge of the desk. "I could have finished up on the Nelson sale. You didn't need to come in."

"That's okay. I also wanted to check on the shipment to Monterey before I left." Calley didn't particularly want to go to her cousin's bridal shower. If she hadn't found a couple of shirts to cover her belly, it would have been out of the question.

"I don't know what I'd do without you. You're not only a good worker, but you did the one thing I swore I'd never allow." She paused. "You became more than an employee. You're a friend. And as such, I want you to know that I plan to buy a crib for that baby of yours."

"That is so nice of you." Calley rose and gave Eva a hug. Her closeness to her boss helped Calley's longing for a stronger relationship with her own sister. Eva kept her from feeling alone.

She sat back down while Eva returned to the kitchen for a snack. "We can put it together when it comes in after in a month or two."

"You're so good to me."

"Would you like something?" Eva pulled a paper towel off the roll.

"No, thanks." Nausea from earlier had finally dissipated, by why take chances?

"You've heard absolutely nothing from Peter about getting his medical history?"

"Nothing. I even tried his cell, but it's disconnected." Calley sighed. "I'm not sure it's worth worrying about."

"Probably not."

Calley opened her top drawer and pulled out the picture. She ran her hand over the cold glass of the photograph. A dark-haired man smiled back at her. "Peter, why did you have to be such a jerk? Worse yet, why didn't I figure it out sooner?"

"Now, don't blame yourself." Eva sat down at her own desk on the other wall of the shop. "My husband had an affair, and I never knew it until the woman called me. It took us years of therapy to regain our trust."

"It's just hard to have new dreams when the old ones died out the way they did."

Calley returned a glimpse back out the window. Their watcher looked up and down the road. What could she want? Calley prayed when she headed to Lincolnville in the next hour, the woman wouldn't follow her.

RILEY OWENS SAT IN the sheriff's cruiser parked, along the side of the old highway. Why'd he agree to be best man? He'd have to give the toast, which meant getting up in front of all those people. The blank paper stared up at him. Maybe he should try for something funny. "Like I've got a sense of humor. I'll just make more of a fool out of myself."

He tugged at his collar. June had just arrived, and the air was already stifling. He could only imagine how hot summer would be.

A blue Nissan Versa whizzed by. According to the radar, it was doing sixty-five in the fifty mile per hour zone. Riley, thankful for the distraction, switched on his lights and siren and pulled out behind it. Less than a mile up, the car jerked into the parking lot of Fred's Diner, the local greasy spoon. It pulled into a spot at the front of the building. Riley used his car to block the vehicle from backing up. A dark-haired woman jumped out of the driver's side door.

"Stop right there." Riley placed his hand on his holster, holding the Glock he carried as he emerged from his vehicle. The brunette didn't look dangerous, but you couldn't be sure.

"I need to use the restroom."

"You'll have to hold it until I get finished."

"I can't." Her hands trembled when she wiped her forehead.

"Too bad." He wrote her tag number down and called it in. The name on the registration information read Calley Regan of Atlanta, Georgia. From the DMV photo, she was the brunette. There were no warrants out for her. Riley figured there was nothing to worry about from the lady, but he'd keep his guard up just in case.

"Good morning, Sheriff. What's new?" Dolly Swenson strolled up behind him. Dolly, a server at Fred's, must have been arriving for the opening shift. The diner was opened for lunch and dinner during the week. It opened for breakfast on the weekend. She lived just a block down and usually walked to work. "Oh, she's a pretty one."

Riley's jaw tightened. "Doesn't matter how pretty they are if they're breaking the law." He pulled his ticket pad from the console in his car.

"You really need to learn how to have fun, Riley. A smart man would find out if she's married, and if not, ask her to lunch." She headed to the woman standing beside the car. "Don't let the old curmudgeon bother you. He sees everything in black or white."

Calley Regan nodded her head and glanced to the road she'd been on. The concern on her face redirected Riley's attention to the street, but no one came or went.

"I need to see your license." He walked up and joined both women. A glance in the driver's side door showed a bottle of water in the console and a pack of opened saltines on the passenger seat.

"Can you write the ticket while I go inside?" Calley handed the license to him. "I promise I won't crawl out the bathroom window."

"This'll take just a minute," he said. Riley wrote up the ticket for speeding. "Sign here." He passed her license back. Dolly continued to watch, obviously disapproving, if her hands on her hips were any indication.

Calley let out a heavy breath and swallowed hard. Her face was pale and sweat covered her forehead. Her hands shook as she signed her name.

"Are you on something?" That would explain her almost paranoid search of Plaskett Drive.

She rolled her eyes. "Prenatal vitamins. And if you don't let me go in, I'm going to throw up all over you."

"I suggest you listen to her, Riley," Dolly said with a laugh. "I know how terrible morning sickness can get, and when you need to hurl, there's no stopping you."

Riley looked into Calley's hazel eyes. "I would think if it were that bad, she'd have stopped sooner. Besides, what kind of mother drives like a maniac and puts her unborn child at risk?"

Calley took a step toward him. "Why you patronizing son of..." She lurched and turned to the side. Not far enough. She threw up on Riley's polished black boots.

"She warned you." Dolly placed an arm around Calley's shoulder. "Come on, dear. Let's get you out of this heat." She paused and turned to Riley. "If you need her, she'll be inside with me. I can't imagine at this point you'd have a problem with that."

Dolly didn't wait for an answer. She led Calley into the diner, out of Riley's view. He shook his left boot. The smell was rancid. He almost thought she'd gotten sick on purpose. That was fine with him. He tore the hefty ticket from the book and slapped it on her windshield.

"I CAN'T BELIEVE I JUST threw up on a cop." Calley shook her head. He wasn't even bad looking. In fact, he was hot. His black cowboy hat sat on top of his forehead. Those dark brown eyes stared down at her, and the day's growth of beard look good on him. His features were strong, from his square jaw to his muscular biceps. She would have enjoyed the view any other time, but the baby had been upsetting her stomach on the hour and a half drive up.

"You really have good timing, don't you?" She talked to the child in her belly.

Country music played from a speaker overhead. Calley sang along. She glanced around the diner while she waited for the woman with the nametag of Dolly to return. Hand-written ads painted on the window announced the special that day. A half pound burger, fries and a coke for three ninety-nine. The thought of that much food made bile rise in Calley's system. She was grateful they hadn't started cooking yet. Greasy food would have only made her feel worse.

She sat off to the right in the first red booth by the door. The vinyl covering was cool to her bare legs. Red stools aligned the counter to her left. Dolly had gone into the back to what Calley assumed was the kitchen area. Voices sounded behind the swinging door. The place reminded her of a small café she'd worked in when she was sixteen. Different color scheme, but same layout.

A black sedan drove past. Calley's hands trembled. She had seen the car in her rearview mirror several times on the interstate. She was sure it had been following her.

"Here you go." Dolly returned from the back room with a cup, drawing Calley's attention from the window. "It's peppermint tea. I drank it when I was pregnant with my second. He gave me a fit during my entire pregnancy." She slid the cup across the table.

"How many kids do you have?" The aroma of mint filled Calley's senses. She drank a sip of the hot liquid.

"Three. All boys." Dolly scooted into the booth across from Calley with a cup of coffee. "This is your first, isn't it?"

"It's obvious I don't know what I'm doing?"

"No, just deductive reasoning. You have no car seat in the back for another kid. What brings you through Lincolnville?"

The tea helped calm Calley's stomach. "My cousin's getting married, and her shower is this weekend."

"My word. You're Lydia's cousin." Dolly patted Calley's hand. "She's just the sweetest thing in the world. No one deserves to be happier than her."

"Yeah." Calley swallowed hard. That's the problem with small towns. Everyone knows everyone else. "Can I ask you a favor?"

"Sure."

"Can you not say anything about the baby? My family doesn't know yet. And seeing as how they're such good Christians, and I'm not married, it's probably not going to go over real big."

"Now don't you worry, I won't tell anyone. And Lydia's a great lady. She isn't the judgmental type."

"It's not Lydia I'm worried about. It's the minister she's marrying."

RILEY FINISHED CLEANING his boots. His mood had gone from bad to worse. He didn't care if Calley Regan was pregnant. He should have locked her up for throwing up on him, if only to confirm his reputation as being cold and heartless. Vomiting on him in front of one of the town gossips didn't help matters. It was probably all over town by now.

"You okay?" BJ stuck her head into his bedroom. "I know you're not thrilled about the people being here for the shower, but it's only the weekend. Then the wedding. After that, you can go back to being the recluse you love to be."

Riley's aunt had a way of being direct with everyone, especially him. She'd raised him after his parents died in a car accident when he was eleven. He brought her up to live after his uncle's death, about six months ago.

"I told you it was fine."

"Your words say fine, but your face has that sourpuss look on it. You need to cheer up, my boy. There should be some nice-looking women at this shower. I understand she's invited her whole sorority from college. If you'd loosen up, you might find one whose company you enjoy."

"I have too much work to worry about chasing after women." Riley didn't want another woman. He hadn't protected the one he'd had before. Why take a chance on losing another?

BJ sat down on the bed. "It's been years since Beth's death. I wish you'd talk to that preacher friend of yours about it so you can move on."

Riley stared at his reflection in the mirror as he adjusted his tie. He had moved on, just not in the way most people thought he should. "I don't need to talk to Matthew about anything. Like you said, it was a long time ago."

"If you say so." A knock on the door interrupted their conversation. "Sounds like our first guests have arrived." She walked from the bedroom and pulled the door partially closed.

BJ's beaming face told of her excitement. She'd probably been bored since she moved from Jacksonville. There certainly were no dinner theatres and the closet large mall was just shy of an hour away. Riley wondered if it was wise uprooting her from her life.

"Well, hello. How are you?" The enthusiasm in BJ's voice carried into the bedroom.

"Hi. You must be BJ. My name's Calley Regan. I think I'm supposed to be here for the weekend."

Riley's stomach bounced. Of all the luck. He glanced through the crack of his opened bedroom door. Her color had returned to her face. He hadn't realized how pretty she was when they'd first met.

"I have two more things in the car," she said.

"You must have planned for every occasion."

"Yeah, I pack a lot. What can I say? I'm a girl." Calley's eyes sparkled.

"A woman can never have too many supplies." BJ gave her a quick hug. "Why don't you bring in the rest? I'll take this one to your room. It's the second on the right."

Riley watched BJ walk into the hallway. He'd found out earlier through the grapevine that he'd given a ticket to Lydia's cousin. That probably wouldn't go over very big since Riley was the best man for her wedding.

Right now, he'd like to find a quick means of escape, but decided Calley should be the one uncomfortable, not him. A fading scent caught his attention when he entered the living room. Calley must have put on perfume before she got to the house. The aroma lingered after she returned outside. At the diner, he hadn't noticed it. He couldn't place the fragrance; he just knew he liked it.

Through the large picture window, he watched Calley head to her car. She glanced up and down the road, definitely looking for someone. Her head followed a black car speeding past. It slowed. She continued to watch. Riley came into full view of the window and the vehicle sped off. Maybe she had a fight with her boyfriend.

He returned his attention to Calley, who tugged a guitar case and another suitcase out of the car's trunk. She shouldn't be carrying those heavy items in her condition.

He sucked in a deep breath and headed for the door.

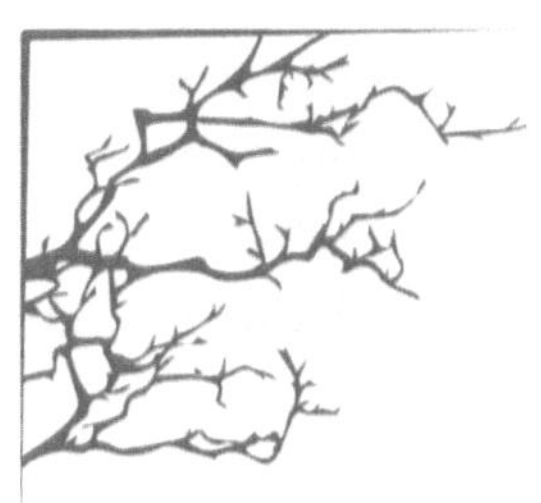

2

Calley's pulse raced. She swore it was the same car she'd seen earlier. Dried mud covered the license plate, making it impossible to get the number, and the windows were darkly tinted. Why would someone follow her all the way here? There was no reason. It couldn't be anyone after the baby. She wasn't even showing yet. There was no money to be had. And Calley certainly didn't make anyone angry on the drive over to cause some sort of road rage.

It was likely her imagination. Maybe she was just being overly protective because of the baby. But she could have sworn it slowed when it came near.

A woodpecker pounded a nearby tree. Calley stared across at the woods. A path led away from the road. She wondered how safe it would be to walk in the mornings. She glanced up the road again. Only if she could find someone to walk with.

She placed her guitar and the suitcase on the ground to close the trunk when the aroma hit her. Sandalwood. She sucked in the fragrance. It reminded her of the hike she took in Australia after graduating college.

"Here, let me get that for you."

Calley jumped at the masculine voice behind her. She spun and found herself face to chest with the sheriff who'd left the ticket on her car earlier.

"I can handle it." She bent to pick up the guitar.

"You shouldn't be carrying all this heavy stuff. At least not in your condition." He wrapped his hand around her fingers on the guitar case.

11

She loosened her grip to dissipate the heat his grip had caused. "By the way, my condition, as you so gently put it, isn't common knowledge. I'd appreciate it not becoming town gossip."

"Not a problem." He glanced down at her stomach. "How far along are you?"

"Twenty weeks."

"You're not showing now, but by the wedding, you will be. Kind of hard to keep it a secret then."

He walked off carrying her belongings. She slammed the lid to the trunk. She hadn't considered that by the wedding she'd be about eight months along. Why couldn't they have had the wedding sooner? Instead, Lydia was waiting for all the family members to be available. There would be no way to hide it by wearing a larger size shirt. How was she going to get up and sing in front of all those people in a church?

"Well, I see you met my nephew." BJ stuck her head out the front door. "After you get settled, would you like some sweet iced tea?"

"Sounds good. And I met your nephew earlier," Calley said. "When he gave me a one hundred eighty-five-dollar ticket."

"I wouldn't have given you a ticket if you hadn't been speeding."

She didn't like the fact he could walk up behind her without her knowing it. "No, you wouldn't have given me a ticket if you weren't a jerk."

BJ laughed. "I think I might have to hide Riley's gun before this weekend is over."

Calley followed Riley back to the bedroom. He didn't say a word as he placed her suitcase at the foot of the queen-size bed and the guitar on top before walking out. Someone covered the bed with a rich blue bedspread. She took the guitar and opened the door to the walk-in closet, setting it inside. The space wasn't as large as hers in Atlanta, but it would be sufficient for a few days.

After getting her clothes hung up, she walked to the large kitchen at the back of the house, where Riley and BJ were preparing dinner. A pony wall separated it from the living-room which held a white stone fireplace. A painting of a deer drinking from a book hung above it. Calley recognized the brown and gold colors–it had to be a Sheryl Coufield painting. The shop had sold a couple and needed more.

Calley loved the layout of the living space. Anyone in the kitchen could see their guests so they wouldn't feel blocked off when they cooked.

A car door shut outside. Calley jumped again. She needed to pull herself together. It was only her imagination that someone had followed her. The person outside the art shop was gone before she left. She must have been waiting for someone. And the person outside her apartment could have been anybody outside her apartment. Same with the one in her rearview mirror. And who passed by outside.

"That must be the other guests." BJ pulled open the door. "Good morning. I believe we're to stay with you." Calley's sister, Allison, glided through the front door. Her five-foot seven-inch thin frame captured Riley's attention. His jaw went slack, and Calley swore he was salivating. Jealously rose in her, yet she didn't know why. Then she saw her mother standing at the opened door. First a ticket, now this.

"Back this way." BJ led Allison inside.

"I'm Allison, and this is my mother, Nanette."

"Nice to meet you." BJ shook Allison's hand.

Calley's eyes met her mother's.

"What are you doing here?" Years of anger showed across her mother's features. The lines around her eyes and her mouth formed a permanent frown. Calley couldn't remember her mother ever smiling.

"It's good to see you too, Mom." Calley didn't bother to smile. There'd been too much history for them to pretend, even in front of strangers.

"I'm surprised to see you here. If you thought this was going to be one of those wild parties you're used to, you're wrong." Her mother spoke in a curt tone. "I guess it's only a matter of time until the whole family finds out what type of daughter I raised."

"Mom, why don't you come back and get settled?" Allison had always been good about distracting her mother for Calley. If not, Calley might have killed her by now. She watched as her sister and BJ led the old woman down the hall.

Calley fought tears welling in her eyes. She could only imagine how much worse this weekend would be if her mother found out about the baby. "You know the worst thing about Jesus?" She spoke to Riley, who stood behind her.

"No. What's that?"

"Christians."

"SMELLS GOOD." RILEY pulled a red potato from the oval serving plate. BJ smacked his hand away. The roast beef sat on the counter. The aroma caused his stomach to grumble.

"You act like you're starving."

"I am. It's been a long day."

"With what? Stopping pretty girls along the side of the road?" She nudged Riley with her elbow. "You'd better be careful. If I didn't know any better, I'd say you found her attractive."

"I find a lot of women attractive." He glanced down at his boot. "I just don't find most as annoying."

"She's got a pretty smile. It's just too bad her eyes don't show it."

"What do you mean?" Riley leaned back against the counter, recalling Calley's eyes. The green sparkled when she spoke about the ticket, yet the brown flecks darkened when her mother walked in.

"There's so much sadness behind them. It's like she needs someone to take her in their arms and tell her she's not alone." BJ sighed. "It shouldn't be that way in a Christian world."

"Well, I have little doubt before she leaves, your arms will be the ones wrapped around her." He kissed BJ's cheek. "From the way you two glared at me earlier over the citation, I have a feeling you'll be fast friends."

"I can't believe you gave her a ticket. I'm assuming she told you she's pregnant?"

Riley's mouth hung opened. "Let me guess. Dolly called you."

"Dolly. What's Dolly got to do with this? I saw her prenatal vitamins on the side of the bed when I took her fresh towels." BJ shook her head. "All alone and with child. I can't imagine how scared she is."

"She has family."

"What? That woman back there? She's loathsome, if you ask me. Walks around with that Bible in her hand like she's the next best thing to Mother Teresa. Too bad she doesn't read it."

"Is there anything I can do to help?" Calley walked up behind the two. "I'm sorry. I didn't mean to interrupt."

"You didn't, child. You can help Riley set the table, then we'll be ready. I'll get the others."

"Do you have to?" Calley smirked, and BJ blurted out a laugh.

Riley pulled plates from the cupboard and handed them to Calley. "Are you going to have any problem with dinner?"

"Why? Are you afraid to sit next to me in case I do?" She grinned. "What happened earlier was an accident. It just sort of came out."

"I'd rather not talk about it."

"Come on." She tapped him on his arm with her fist. "That's going to make a great story to tell your grandkids one day."

"I doubt I have to worry about that. I'm just surprised it's not all over town since it happened in front of Dolly." Irritation rose as Riley imagined the laughs he'd get from the locals over a woman throwing up on him.

"I asked her not to say anything about... you know." She finished placing the last plate on the table.

"If you don't want anyone to know, I suggest you keep your pills out of sight. BJ saw them on your nightstand earlier."

The murmur of small talk drifted into the room. Nanette strolled into the eat-in-kitchen, followed by Allison.

"I just hope it's not going to upset my stomach." Nanette was saying. "Certain foods give me indigestion, and I'd hate to be uncomfortable during the party tomorrow."

"I think everything will be fine." BJ held her smile. "If you need anything special, I'll be more than happy to fix it."

Nanette stopped short when she saw Calley. Her lips creased to a straight line, and she shook her head at her daughter. "Where do you want me to sit?"

"Why don't you sit here, Mom?" Allison led her mother to a chair at the oval table.

They sat on one side, Calley opposite them. Riley took a seat at the head of the table. He noticed BJ took a chair next to Calley, not at the other end of the table. It was her way of making sure Calley wasn't alone. Some days, he wished he had that caring Christian nature. But it was hard to care for others when they wouldn't be in your life very long.

CALLEY PLAYED WITH her fork, pushing her corn around the flowered plate. The roast was so tender it fell apart with her fork. It practically melted in her mouth. She wanted more meat, but didn't want to look like a pig. Especially since she still had other food left. No one talked while they ate. Calley couldn't stand the silence. She liked chatter, but she wasn't about to start it for fear her mother would take anything she said and make a scene from it.

"So, Allison," BJ finally spoke. "What is it you do in Augusta?"

"I'm a nurse."

"Good for you. That's a fine profession. Isn't it, Riley?"

Riley glanced up. His fork full of potatoes stopped in midair. "Yes, it is."

Calley stifled the laugh. She took a drink of her iced tea. She knew a matchmaker when she saw one. BJ and Eva would get along well.

"Do you specialize in a certain type of medicine?" BJ continued.

"I work for a pediatrician."

"Isn't that something, Riley?"

"Yeah, it's something." He glowered at his aunt.

"Better you than me," Calley whispered under her breath.

"Well, Nanette, you must be proud of your daughter. Being a nurse is quite a feat."

"I am." She patted Allison's arm. "She's near perfect." Nanette then glared across the table at Calley.

Calley rolled her eyes and leaned back in her chair. Allison was always the perfect child, getting straight A's and taking care of her parents. Calley, on the other hand, liked to have fun. Grades were never that important. She'd barely squeaked by in high school and only went to college to learn more about art and to get a business degree.

"From what I've seen of both your girls, you have a lot to be proud of. One a nurse, the other a businesswoman. And soon to be a mother."

Nanette's fork dropped on her plate. "What?" Her eyes barreled toward Calley like a semi-truck at full speed.

Calley's heart leapt as she thought of what to say to calm the situation. Nothing came to her, so she just said, "Surprise."

"I'm sorry," BJ said. "I just assumed she knew."

"I can't believe you. And then you come here just to show off what type of woman you are."

Calley's face warmed.

"You and your wild ways. Good thing your father's gone, or this would have sent him to his grave for sure." Nanette rose from her seat, her fists white. "Why couldn't you be good like your sister or cousin, Lydia? Everyone else in the family has good, godly children. I imagine your grandfather is rolling over in his grave."

"I imagine he's in heaven with Jesus enjoying himself, but you think what you want," Calley said. Why did her grandfather have to be a minister? It only made living up to the Pendleton name worse.

"I just wish there was something I could be proud of." Her mother threw her napkin onto her plate. "I can't eat any more. I need to lie down."

"I'll take you, Mom." Allison rose and glanced down at Calley with a grimace.

Calley crossed her arms over her chest and leaned back. She watched Allison guide her mother out of the room as if she were too much of an invalid to walk by herself. Her mother was anything but old. Once they were out of sight, she said, "Aren't family get-togethers fun?"

"Totally." Riley took a bite of potato, as if unfazed by the tension in the air.

Calley's appetite had dissipated. She was never good enough for her mother. And no matter how much she'd love to be the prodigal, she knew it would never happen. Her mother would never welcome her home. Especially not after what she did to her Uncle Joe. So why did she care so much?

RILEY WIPED HIS FOREHEAD. Even evenings were too warm out in this old garage. The air from the A/C coming in from the opened door of the kitchen did little to cool things off.

He removed the carburetor from the bike, careful not to tear the intake boot. He wasn't sure he'd ever get the 1981 Yamaha XS 650 running, but it gave his mind a break from work. It'd been slow finding parts and getting down to the dirty work, but he hoped to have it running within the next couple of weeks.

A shuffle of feet inside the kitchen caught his attention. Everyone had gone to their rooms not too long after that uncomfortable dinner. Nanette's angry words still shocked him. How Calley turned out with a sense a humor was beyond him.

He smiled, recalling how his aunt tried to get him to notice Allison. She and Calley looked similar with their green eyes and dark hair. However, Allison had at least two inches on Calley, and she was quiet while Calley fidgeted the entire meal. As hard as BJ tried to get his attention on Allison, all Riley could do was look at Calley. Maybe what they say is true, opposites attract. Not that anything would come from the attraction. He'd found out years ago what falling in love could do to your heart and soul. He'd never find himself in that position again. His job was to protect this community, and he couldn't do that if he had to worry about a woman, not to mention one with a child.

Whoever it was in the outer room scooted something on the buffet below the front window. No lights shown from inside the house.

Riley walked to the open doorway and saw the figure standing at the window. Calley. Maybe the baby was giving her a hard time. She stared out the window, turning her head back and forth. She was looking for someone. Maybe she called her boyfriend to come meet her.

"It's not a smart thing to wander around in the dark in a cop's house. You could find yourself in a dangerous situation." Riley came through the kitchen and into the living room.

Her hair was in disarray, and she wore a pair of floral pajama pants and a t-shirt. A floral scent came from her direction. He had to admit, she smelled as good as she looked.

"I'm sorry. I couldn't sleep and didn't want to wake anyone." She ran her eyes up and down him, then laughed. "Been playing in grease?"

"I'm restoring an old motorcycle." He walked to the curtain and glanced out of a one-inch opening. "So, who are you looking for?"

"What makes you think I'm looking for anyone?" She headed to the kitchen. The quiver in her voice betrayed her.

"I figured you called someone to come get you away from here. If you want to go out, BJ and I won't care. You can keep the front door unlocked so you can get back in."

"I didn't call anyone. And if I wanted to go out, I'd go." She threw her shoulders back. "Whether it bothered you or not."

He couldn't help but think that if it bothered him, she'd make a point of going out. She reminded him of a teenager. Doing the opposite of what was expected.

"I was just looking outside. That's all." She opened the refrigerator and stared inside.

"Now, if someone's following you, I'd be the best person to stop it. We don't get many strangers around here, so I could have my people keeping an eye out."

She let out a heavy breath. "Except it could be my imagination. I just think someone is out there watching me. When I turned off the highway in Calhoun to get something to drink, a dark vehicle followed. I thought I saw it drive when I got here."

"And you don't know who it is or what they want?" Anger rose in Riley at some stranger causing her concern. She had enough to worry about with the baby.

"No. But it's a good thing there's no one to worry about me. 'Cause if the person doesn't stop, I can run away to some place I can't be found."

CATCH YOUR BREATH

COOL AIR FROM THE AIR conditioner blew Calley's hair and caused a slight chill. She walked to the sliding glass door and opened it to allow some warmth from outside to hit her. Rain scented the night air and a flash of lightning glowed in the distance. Insects droned like a chorus where each had their own song.

She recalled having to catch her breath when she heard the noise behind her. That it was Riley should have put her mind more at ease, but it didn't. If he could be this quiet and catch her off guard, so could someone else. His t-shirt stretched across his chest as he stood in the light from the garage. He needed a shave, but the whiskers looked good on him. It gave her yearnings she hadn't had in a while.

"You shouldn't run away." Riley washed the grease from his hands in the kitchen sink. "I'll give you my card. If you see this car again, call me or try to get his tag number. I'll check him out."

"Thanks. Watch it be some old geezer. You'll give him a heart attack, being all serious like you are."

She turned to walk away, but Riley grabbed hold of her arm, and she fell toward him. His breath brushed against her face.

"If you thought he was some geezer, you wouldn't be worried. Just let me know if you see him."

She wanted to run her hand over his chest and have those muscular arms hold her. She gave her head a shake to send the thoughts away. Boy, this baby must be making her hormones go wonkers. She needed to get out of there before she made a fool of herself.

"I will. Thanks again." She hoped her quick gait wasn't too noticeable, but she needed to get away from this man. He was making her body feel things she didn't want to feel.

Calley glanced down at her belly. "Besides, no one needs to worry about us. I'll take care of you, and as long as you're safe, it doesn't really matter what the guy might want."

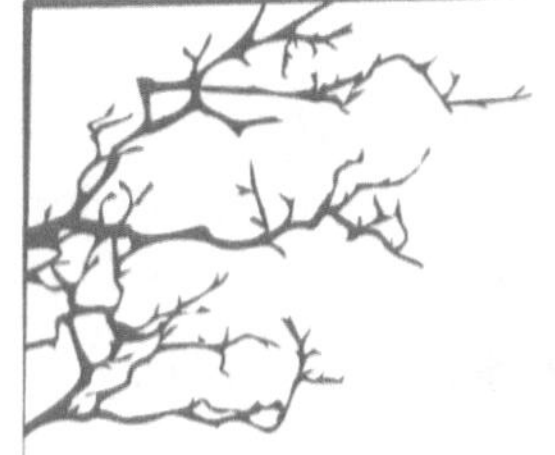

3

Riley pulled up to the house for lunch. Loud music came from inside. Tommy James, if he recalled. He smiled. His mom used to play their music all the time. He found Calley in the kitchen. She bounced up and down to the music as she rinsed dishes in the sink.

She hopped around singing to "I Think We're Alone Now" oblivious to the fact he watched her. Her bare feet slapped against the wood floor. Could all that dancing be good for the baby? If nothing else, she seemed in a better mood than the night before.

Calley spun and stopped in her tracks. At first, fear filled her eyes, but it was short-lived. She stared at Riley, then without missing a note, danced up to him, singing along with the words. She had a great voice. It's no wonder Lydia asked her to sing at the wedding. Calley had done her hair up in a ponytail, and it swung back and forth. The aroma of dishwashing soap drifted into Riley's nostrils.

She grabbed his shoulder and sang into his ear. Her ponytail tickled his face. Her hair felt soft, at least what he could feel of it. She pulled his hat off his head and placed it on her own. It slid to her eyes. She danced over to the stereo, and as the song faded, she pressed the OFF button.

"Do you always sneak up on people like that?" Calley panted as she spoke.

"I don't usually find people dancing around my house." He walked over and took his hat off her head and placed it on the sideboard. "Where's everyone else?"

"As usual, my mom waited until the last moment to buy a gift for the shower. So BJ drove them to Chattanooga. "She pulled at her t-shirt, drenched with sweat. "I guess I need to take a shower."

23

"Is it healthy for you to move around like that?"

"The doctor says to stay active, so I don't gain a bunch of weight. Unless they tell me different or it feels wrong, I'll dance until this kid drops." She walked to the corner of the hallway and stopped. "What's wrong, Sheriff? Are you afraid you might have to deliver this baby?"

"No. I'm just wondering who's more of a flake, you or Lydia's friend Sheryl." He shook his head.

"Sheryl's fun, not a flake. And I think we've both been insulted." She pointed an index finger at him. "You will pay for that in the end."

He couldn't take his eyes off her as she walked away. The grin remained on his face. It was the first time in a long time he felt this good.

CALLEY BOUNCED HER hand against the steering wheel to the music. How could anyone not feel good when music's playing? She recalled the look on Riley's face while he watched her dance. From the sparkle in his eyes, he seemed to enjoy it. Too bad he didn't dance with her. It'd be nice to have someone to loosen up with. But he had done nothing more than give her a quick smile. Why was he such a stick in the mud? A guy that good looking should be out having fun with a bunch of women chasing him around.

"I'll get him to laugh before I leave. You just watch." She patted her stomach.

Calley pulled into the parking, paused, and stared at the vast church. The light-colored brick, large white columns, and bell tower made a striking scene against the blue backdrop of the sky. She opened her door and dragged herself from the car. Before taking a step, she looked up. "Please God, don't strike me down once I enter." She pulled her floral blouse down, hoping to cover any growing bulge.

Red and blue streamers and balloons decorated the room for the wedding shower. Barbeque pork stood in a warmer off to the side. The smell overwhelmed Calley. She'd been hungry all morning, and her stomach wanted even more food. If she kept this up, she'd weigh a ton by the time the baby arrived.

Almost every table was full. BJ waved. Great. Calley had been hoping to find a table in the back where she could go unnoticed.

"Calley," Sheryl Coufield shouted. She and Lydia Frederickson rushed up and pulled her into a hug. Lydia's silk shirt was soft against Calley's arm. "I wasn't sure you were going to make it."

"Things were slow at the shop." Calley turned to Sheryl. "By the way, we need to get together so you can give me some more paintings. You're sold out again."

"No problem." Sheryl pushed her blonde hair to one side. "I love to be in demand."

All three women laughed and hugged each other again.

"And how's the soon-to-be married woman?" An edge came over Calley. Now that she was here, she wasn't sure she wanted to see her perfect cousin. Perfect not only in looks but in her walk with God. She was the person her grandfather would be most proud of if he were still alive.

"I'm doing wonderful. Looking forward to getting this over with." Lydia's violet eyes shined in the overhead lights.

"Looking forward to the honeymoon, are we?"

When Lydia blushed, the tension in Calley disappeared. It was still easy to tease her cousin.

"Well, I need to run off and chit-chat with the others," Lydia said. "Stick around later. I'd love to have time to catch up."

Calley was glad for everything going right in Lydia's life. So much had happened to her in the last couple of years. Her husband, Justine, died, and then a couple of years later someone tried to killer her. She deserved to be happy. Calley wondered when it would be her turn. She shook her head to get her thoughts back to the party. The last thing she wanted was for people to think she took after her grouchy mother.

"We're sitting over here." Sheryl directed Calley to BJ's table. Unfortunately, Allison and Nanette were there as well.

"So'd you get what you needed in Chattanooga?" Calley said as she and Sheryl approached.

"We got her a wok," Allison said. "We have one at the house and love it."

"Great." Calley held up her bag. "I went for something sexy."

"Thank goodness. I thought I'd be the only one." Sheryl squeezed her hand. "So, how are you enjoying your stay with Riley?"

"He's way too solemn for someone so good-looking."

"The wedding isn't improving his disposition, either. I think being the best man and having to give a toast is making him worse. I told him I'd write it for him, but I don't think he trusts me." Sheryl laughed.

"I'm not sure I would either." Calley elbowed her. "I can only imagine what you'd say."

"It wouldn't be bad. At least it'd be funny." Sheryl winked. "Maybe we can get him to loosen up a bit later. He and some groomsmen are going to stop by."

"Any you're interested in?" Calley nudged Sheryl with her hip.

"Alas, I think I'm destined to be a lone woman with a house full of cats." Sheryl swept her arm across her forehead.

"Except you're allergic to cats," Calley said. "What about Riley? He's single."

"I'd have to shoot him. He's wound too tight."

"I don't think anything could loosen that man up." Calley poured some punch from a nearby pitcher. She took a sip of the too sour mixture. "Like I said, he's so serious."

"It wouldn't bother you to be a bit more serious." Nanette scowled up at Calley. "It might keep you from getting into all these messes you get into." She gave a quick look at Calley's midsection.

Calley rolled her eyes at her mother. Every party has a pooper.

"Listen." Sheryl tugged Calley's attention away. "Later on, would you like to head over to the house and look at what I have available for the shop? Lydia can meet us, and we can catch you up on the gossip."

"Let me know when." Calley was always grateful for Sheryl's distraction. It seemed she had a sixth sense when trouble brewed.

RILEY PULLED INTO THE parking lot of the church. Why did he have to come to the shower? Wasn't that for women? Matthew Winters' motorcycle rumbled in the distance. Riley waited. If the groom could be late, so could the best man.

He nodded in Matthew's direction when he pulled up beside the sheriff's cruiser. Riley waited until Matthew had the helmet off. Two other members of the party arrived within seconds. Riley opened the car door, the humidity blasting him.

"So, when are you going to get that Yamaha of yours done so you can stop supporting those oil companies with that car of yours?" Matthew's smile was wide as he stepped from the bike. Sweat ran down his forehead and his hair lay flat from his helmet he removed. "In this heat, the last thing I want to go without is air conditioning." He let Matthew lead the way. "Tell me again how Lydia talked you into this?"

"What can I say?" Matthew said. "I'm in love. You should try it someday."

Riley allowed Matthew and the others to enter first. The air conditioner blasted cool air. People murmured and moved about. A long sheet cake lay on the table as he entered. The white frosting held blue and red roses. Three women rushed up to ask if he was hungry. Good thing he'd grabbed a sandwich at home, or he'd have to accept. Being one of the few single men in Lincolnville made him a prime target for the single women. They didn't understand he had no interest in having a family. The memory of Calley in the kitchen flashed into his mind. His heart stepped up its tempo.

"Hey Riley." Marylou Tyson sauntered up to him. She was the most forceful in her attraction to him. She'd come to the station at least twice a week to see him. Since she moved to town four months prior, he'd tried to clarify that they were just friends, but she didn't listen. "I made the fried okra you like so much. Would you like me to get you a plate?" She gave him a coy grin. There was nothing demure about this woman. Every time Riley entered a room she was in, her eyes cast a gaze similar to that of a piranha staring at a goldfish. Hers were the last clutches he wanted to find himself in.

"Thanks, but I just had a sandwich." Riley rushed around her, hoping he didn't appear rude. Marylou's perfume was harsh. It didn't entice him. It attacked him.

"The men are here," Sheryl yelled.

Riley's cheeks warmed. Why did she have to draw attention to them? His eye caught sight of Calley seated beside her. She looked like she was having a good time as she wiggled her fingers in the air at him.

He nodded and sucked in an extra breath.

"Matthew." Lydia waved her fiancé over. The other men followed like lemmings. Riley wondered where the nearest cliff was that they'd all soon be jumping off.

When they arrived at the table, Lydia introduced them to her aunt and cousins. Matthew spoke for a moment with everyone before getting to Calley. Riley tossed his hat from hand to hand. He tried to divert his attention, but the brown colors in Calley's blouse made her eyes stand out. She really was beautiful.

"It's nice to meet you." Matthew had a welcoming smile on his face as he greeted Calley. "I understand you work for an art shop in Atlanta. At least someone keeps Sheryl busy."

"Someone's got to," Riley said.

"Ooh. That almost sounded like a joke." Calley laughed. "I didn't know you had it in you. Did someone not put enough starch in that collar of yours?"

Riley didn't respond. He knew he was too serious. But this woman appeared to be way too carefree. Especially since she was having a child.

Sheryl stood and tapped her glass with a fork. "Now that the groom has arrived, my good friend and Lydia's cousin, Calley Regan has agreed to sing a song in honor of the lucky couple."

People clapped as Calley climbed the few steps to the stage. She strapped her guitar around her shoulder and sat on a stool in the center.

Riley walked to the back, poured himself some tea, and leaned against the wall. He swallowed down the ice, hoping to cool himself down. He wasn't sure if he was hot from the temperature or from staring at Calley. It'd been a while since a woman caught his attention that way she had.

She sang "Time in a Bottle." A classic, but a good one. When she finished, everyone stood and applauded. She was quite good. Matthew shook her hand, and Lydia hugged her. Riley seemed to be the only one who noticed tears welling in Calley's eyes as she made her way to the front door.

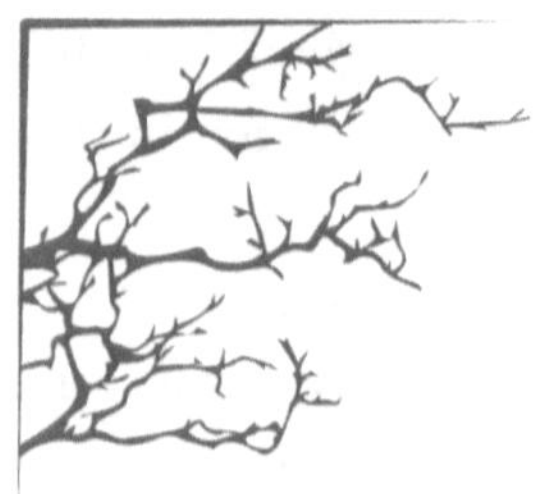

4

How could she allow herself to get so emotional because of a song? It had to be her hormones. No, it was because she missed Peter. Why did he have to be married? A salty tear dribbled to Calley's lips. The door swung open and cool air from inside floated over her.

"Are you all right?" Allison placed a hand on her shoulder. "You looked like you were ready to cry."

"I just needed some air. I've had morning sickness, and it was a bit much in there," Calley said. A bead of perspiration tickled as it made its way down her back.

"I hate you being sick at a celebration for Lydia." Concern filled Allison's eyes. "Are you sure you're up to this, especially for the wedding?"

Here it comes. She spun to face her sister. "Let me guess. Mom has a message for me."

"You know how she is. She knows your pregnancy will be showing by the wedding, and she hates for you to have to face all the gossip."

"She doesn't give a rat's behind about me. She doesn't want everyone to know her daughter's a *jezebel*." Calley's mother couldn't wait to use the Biblical name for her.

"Don't talk like that."

"Why not? She does."

"I don't feel that way." Allison stepped closer to Calley.

"Give me a break." Calley crossed her arms, turned away from her sister, and leaned against a pillar. "You two probably have a good time with all the gossiping you do about me."

"You really don't see it, do you?" Allison's voice was low.

30

"See what?"

"How lucky you are you got away."

"Got away." Calley faced her sister. "You make it sound like it's a prison, and you have yet to escape."

"Some days I feel like it is." Allison's lips tightened.

"You can leave, too." Calley recalled how close she and her sister had been when they were younger. Once Allison entered high school, that all changed. She no longer wanted to have her goofy, little sister hanging around when she was vying for prom queen.

"Who'll take care of her?" Allison looked toward the closed door. A pained expression held on her face.

"Our mother is not helpless. She can take care of herself. Maybe you don't leave because you're afraid of what's out there." Calley stared out at the parking lot. "BJ was trying to get you and Riley together. You have a lot in common with your strong work ethic and all." She didn't add that both were also sticks-in-the-mud.

"I don't know. He seems too quiet. I'd like someone to wake me up."

"What are you trying to do, give Mom a heart attack?"

Both women laughed.

"No. I just want to be loved."

"You will be. All you have to do is put yourself out there." Calley continued to lean on the column on the front porch of the church. "And tell Mom not to worry. I have no intention of coming to the wedding. Lydia's one of the few people who has always treated me good. I don't think I could stand the look of condemnation in her eyes."

RILEY STOOD INSIDE, glancing at the door. He wanted to check on Calley, but her sister had bolted up and headed out first. He'd been so distracted he hadn't seen Marylou head in his direction.

"I haven't seen you eat anything," she said. "Would you like me to get you a plate?"

"I'm fine."

"So how are you handling all that company at your house?" Marylou placed her hands behind her back and stood with one foot in front of the other. The red dress she wore was a perfect fit across her body, down to her knees. However, her makeup was as overdone as her perfume. And if she trimmed her eyebrows one more time, they'd be gone.

"I'm making do," Riley said. The front door opened, and Allison returned inside. Calley didn't follow. "If you'll excuse me for a minute, please."

The sun beat down on him as he walked onto the front porch. It was like going from a refrigerator to the oven within seconds. Calley leaned on one of the large columns outside.

"It's too warm to be standing out here. You might get dehydrated."

She looked up at him with a smirk. "Since when did you become my mother?"

"I'm just making sure you take care of yourself. I wouldn't want to have to take you to the hospital. It'd be hard to keep your secret with flashing red lights."

"Don't worry. I won't let anything happen to the baby." Calley touched her stomach.

"Good." Riley stared out at the street. Calley's perfume reminded him of a flower alone in a field. Not strong, but subtle and nice. "You sounded good in there. It takes a lot to impress Matthew, but you did."

"It's too bad I won't be here to sing at the wedding," Calley said.

"Why not?" Riley took a step back. "I thought you agreed."

Disappointed rushed in that the wedding wasn't sooner. She loved to sing, and he enjoyed listening to her. Unfortunately, Lydia's parents would be out of town until the day before. The shower had been months early to accommodate other family member's schedules.

"What minister wants an unmarried pregnant woman standing up in front of his congregation singing about true love?"

"Matthew isn't that way. He had a crazy life before he became a minister, and he's not one to pass judgment."

"Yeah. Well, he needs to tell my mother and all the other good Christian people out there."

"I have a feeling you judge all Christians based on your mother's actions. Let me tell you something about that woman. She's judgmental and hypocritical. Not a very good Christian, if you ask me." He leaned a hand above Calley's head on the column. Maybe he should have kept his mouth shut.

"Apparently no one told you it wasn't proper to talk bad about a Southern woman's mother."

"I'm sorry. But I don't think a good Christian woman would talk to her child the way she did you last night."

"Boy, when you get going, you get really excited, don't you?" Calley looked down at the ground. "And what about you, Riley Owens? Are you a good Christian?"

"Not as good as I should be. But we all have our hang-ups."

She turned to face him. "Yeah, we do, don't we?"

Riley touched her face. He wondered if she realized how pretty she was, and how inviting her lips were. He wanted to kiss her, but he wasn't sure if she could be receptive.

At once, the door opened, and Marylou walked out.

"Oh, I'm sorry, I didn't mean to interrupt." She gave a quick glare Calley's way before she disappeared back inside.

Before he could apologize for his actions, fear entered Calley's eyes.

"It's him." She grasped Riley's arm as her eyes locked over his shoulder. "It's the guy in the black car."

"Get back inside." He patted her hand, then jumped two steps at a time as he raced toward his cruiser.

RILEY SPED AFTER THE sedan. The sheriff's car, a Dodge Charger, was doing over a hundred, and the Lexus was about to lose him.

"Sylvi," Riley yelled into his radio, "I need backup on Hinden Road. A black Lexus IS, four-door sedan. Something's covering the tag. I'm heading north. Get me backup heading south."

"I'll send someone right over." Sylvi, the office clerk, had an edge to her voice.

The Lexus disappeared at a fork in the road. Riley skidded to a stop. He got out and listened. A dog howled in the distance.

They had nothing to go on but a black Lexus. That wasn't much, in an area where wealthy people lived. He leaned back on the hood; angry he hadn't kept his eyes opened. He might have spotted the car first and been able to stop it, but Calley had drawn his attention. She seemed to do that a lot lately. It might be good for her to leave tomorrow. He'd be able to get his mind back on work.

Deputy Green drove up from the right.

"I lost him." Riley pulled his hat off and wiped his forehead. The guy was obviously following Calley. Otherwise, why run?

"Who was he?" Deputy Green spoke through his open window.

"I don't know. He was speeding." Riley saw no need to say anything further at this point. "We need to keep an eye out."

Deputy Green nodded and pulled away. His tires threw dirt into the dry air.

Riley returned to his car and sat staring up and down the road. He couldn't save Beth six years ago. And now, there was another woman in his life in danger. He slapped the steering wheel. There was no way he'd allow anything to happen to Calley on his watch.

CALLEY COULDN'T FOCUS. Why hadn't Riley called? She strolled back to the sanctuary and sat in a back pew. She ran her hand over the soft fabric on the seat. A large wooden cross hung in the front. It had been a gift to the church from her uncle, Lydia's father. Their grandfather had helped build the church. Everyone in her family was a good Christian. Everyone but her.

How was it you could sit in a room full of people and yet feel all alone? Her lip quivered.

"Calley?" Lydia's voice sounded behind. "Are you all right?"

"Yeah. I just needed a break."

Lydia sat next to her. "Is there something wrong? You look pale."

"I haven't been feeling well, but I didn't want to miss the shower."

"I'm glad you didn't. Nothing serious, I hope."

"No. I've just had a hard time lately. I'm thinking of moving out to the West Coast. If so, I'm not sure I can sing at your wedding." She didn't have the heart to tell her cousin the real reason. "I'm sorry. I know I agreed." A sob escaped her.

"What's really going on? Did you break up with that guy you were seeing?"

"He dumped me."

"I'm so sorry." She lifted Calley's chin. "But you can't let him mess up your life. You need to hold your head high. Show him what he's missing."

"It's hard when I thought we were going to be forever. This weekend is just reminding me." Calley wiped at her cheek. "I think need to get someone else to sing. Just in case I can't be here."

"I'll think about it, but not for a while. We'll talk and see if you don't feel better in a couple of weeks." Lydia pulled Calley into a hug. "I'm sorry you're hurting."

Calley stayed with Lydia's arms around her for a few more minutes. "I think we might want to get back to the party before people think you've deserted them," Calley said.

"Let them wonder. Right now, you're more important."

"I have a feeling you being the guest of honor, they'd argue that." Calley rose. "Besides, I will not have you hiding and sulking with me on a day of celebration."

They walked out, arms hooked around each other. Riley stood in the corner. He gave Calley a quick nod when she looked his way.

She headed in his direction. "Let me guess, an old geezer who just bought a new car."

"Let's go somewhere we can talk."

Riley's voice held an ominous tone. It did little to make Calley feel better. She followed him to the reception area. "If you're trying to worry me, this is the way to do it."

"We didn't catch him. But one thing's for sure. He didn't want the police to stop him." Riley placed a hand on her shoulder. "I'm not sure it's a good idea for you to go back home."

"Where shall I go? It's not like I have an abundance of options." She glanced out the window. There was no other choice. "I'll let the police know when I get back to Atlanta. Can they call you if they need to?"

"Yes. Just be careful. We don't know what this guy wants."

Calley nodded. Something inside told her what he wanted. She touched her stomach. Never would she allow anything to happen to her child. She'd die first.

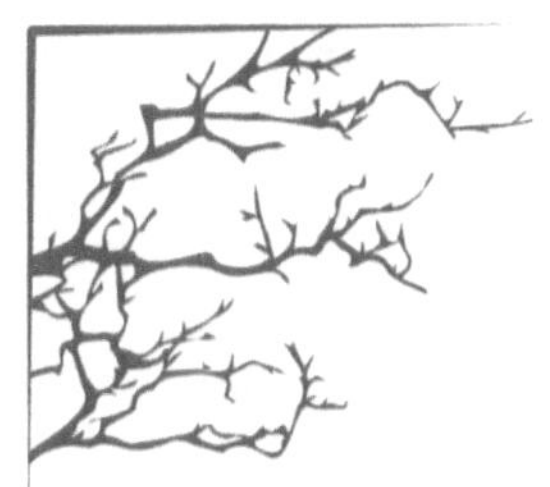

5

Calley heaved the suitcase off the bed. How was she going to fit two bags and a guitar in the back of her car when she had Sheryl's paintings taking up so much space? She'd just have to cram the bags on the floor in the back. The guitar could sit up front.

Disappointment had rushed in when Riley hadn't been there to say goodbye when she got up for breakfast. BJ told her an accident took him away early that morning. Her mother and Allison sat in the dining room when she came out. BJ washed dishes at the kitchen sink.

"I think I have everything," Calley said.

BJ walked over to her and pulled her into a hug. "Don't you be a stranger, child. You make sure you answer my calls, or I'll come down there to that big city looking for you."

She touched Calley's cheek, a small gesture, but it warmed Calley inside. She looked over at her mother, but the woman didn't even glance her way. Calley shrugged it off.

Allison stood and walked toward her. "Here, let me help you with those." She grabbed one of the cases and led Calley out.

"Oh, no." Allison gasped.

Calley's tires were flat. "You'd better check your car, too," Calley said.

Allison walked to her Lincoln. "No. It looks like it's just yours." She shook her head and stared at the tires. "They're flat on this side, also."

Calley placed her belongings inside the car and returned inside and called the auto club. Someone would be by within thirty minutes.

"It must have been kids, pulling a prank." BJ poured Calley some sweet iced-tea. "Maybe Riley walked out before they had time to do any

37

damage to the other cars." She pulled her cellphone from her pocket. "I'll give him a call."

"No, I don't want to bother him when he's dealing with a car accident. It's just some prank, I'm sure."

"Probably more like someone you made mad," Nanette said. "If you treated people right, then this wouldn't happen."

Calley was looking for the right words to tell her mother off when BJ spoke.

"I haven't seen Calley treat anyone with anything but kindness and respect." BJ stood against a counter in the kitchen. She placed her hands on her hips and set her jaw tight. "I imagine it was a couple of boys who were going to do all the cars. Riley got an early call. Probably when they saw his bedroom light come on, they took off."

Calley would miss BJ. They'd become good friends in only a couple of days. As much as she hated to admit it, she'd miss Riley as well. She wondered if he'd miss her, too? He'd sat beside her during the shower, talking, watching everyone alone with her. Of course, it could have been to get a better look at Allison who sat across from them.

Calley sighed. It didn't really matter. She'd probably never see him again.

"Excuse me. I should let my boss know I'll be late." Calley walked into the living room near the fireplace and called Eva. She explained what had happened and that she'd be about two hours behind, if she was lucky.

"You're not stuck at some repair shop, are you?" Eva crunched on what Calley assumed was a potato chip. They were Eva's weakness.

"No. I saw them when I first got ready to leave. I'm still at BJ's."

"Good. I wonder if I shouldn't thank them for taking such good care of you."

Calley laughed. "I have three new Coufield paintings to drop by."

"It can wait until tomorrow. I don't want you overdoing it." Eva had been Calley's biggest supporter once she found out about the baby.

"I'm fine."

A knock on the door announced the mechanic.

"I've got to go. I'll see you soon."

Within an hour, she was standing by her car, ready to leave. The mechanic had brought four tires that fit on her car, keeping her from having to wait any longer. In the city, she'd have to have waited all day if not overnight for them to get the tires in.

"You have yourself a safe trip, child." BJ pulled Calley into another hug. "Call me or send a text or something when you get home, so I know you made it."

"I will."

"Are you sure you don't want something for the road home? I could fix you a sandwich."

"No. I'll be fine." She didn't want BJ to go to any more trouble, so she planned to stop and get some fruit on her way out. It wasn't a very long drive, but the way the baby acted, you'd think it never got fed.

BJ and Allison stood on the porch and watched her leave. Nanette probably still sat at the dining room table.

Two miles up the road, Calley pulled into the parking lot of Lou's grocery. Inside, she took in the aroma of fresh bread. To get to the fruit, she had to bypass the bakery department. Not simple task when you're not pregnant. In her condition, it was almost impossible.

She picked up a red apple, then set it back down and stared down at the green ones. They all looked good, just not as good as a chocolate-covered donut from the bakery. She fought her temptation, telling herself the donut wasn't healthy for the baby.

"You look like a woman with a decision to make."

Calley startled at the female voice behind her. She turned and faced a woman in an expensive tan suede jacket and nice suede boots. Calley almost dropped the apple from her grip. This was the woman watching her at work. She looked to be in her forties with gray eyes and brown hair cut into a pixie. Her face was line free. Calley assumed from either a facelift or Botox.

"I'd rather have something from the bakery, but I'm trying to fight it," she said. Her pulse pounded in her ears, and her mouth had gone dry.

"Maybe you should try some self-control." The woman took a step closer, causing Calley to back into the fruit stand. "Then you wouldn't sleep with married men."

The breath escaped Calley. "Who are you?"

"Oh, come on now. Peter didn't show you any family snapshots.

Calley stared at the woman. What do you say about something like this? "I didn't know." Her knees weakened, and her stomach lurched. *Please don't let me throw up on this woman.*

"Well, you do now." The woman's jaw clenched, and her voice lowered. "If you think you'll get my husband to leave me, think again. I know how to take care of women like you." She looked Calley up and down and gave her a sneer.

Calley's heart pounded in her chest. She grabbed two red apples and skirted around the woman. She breathed a sigh of relief when Peter's wife didn't follow. What if she waited for her outside? Calley dawdled longer than necessary in the hopes there would be no surprises waiting in the parking lot.

After wasting ten minutes inside the store, Calley paid for the apples and a strawberry tart to tide her over on the drive home. When she unlocked her car door, she spotted the black Lexus she'd seen following her before. The expensive vehicle went well with Mrs. Jameson's jacket. Calley sat in her car for what seemed like hours before starting it and heading home. How could she have been so stupid as to get involved with a married man?

RILEY SAT IN THE CRUISER, parked on Plaskett Road. He glanced down at the blank paper. No words came to his mind. If he didn't come up with something, there'd be no toast at the wedding. Maybe he should take Sheryl up on her offer, cutting out the things he didn't want to say. He should head back to the office and not fret over it for a while. There were still months until the wedding. Unfortunately, he was one to get things done way ahead of time or he'd worry until it was complete. He continued to sit.

He knew why he didn't leave. Calley would have to pass this way to get to the interstate. He hadn't gotten a chance to say goodbye. He'd have to settle for watching her leave.

Within minutes, Calley's blue car whizzed past, faster than it should have. Riley caught himself smiling. There'd be no ticket, just a goodbye. He was ready to go after her, when he caught sight of a black Lexus a few seconds behind her. Riley allowed it to pass then flipped on his lights and siren before taking off after it. This time, the car pulled to the side of the road just before the on-ramp to the interstate.

Riley got a good look at the plate. The day before, it had been obscured, but his gut told him this was the same car. He called it in. The car was registered to a Peter and Fifi Jameson. Riley paused before stepping from his vehicle. The window of the Lexus rolled down as he approached.

"How can I help you, officer?" The female driver sat with her hands on the steering wheel. Large jeweled white sunglasses covered her eyes, and the rings on her fingers screamed rich.

"We have an all points out for a black Lexus. I need to see your license."

"Here you go." She handed over both her license and a business card. It showed the name of Peter Jameson, Attorney at Law in Atlanta.

The embossed card did little to impress Riley. "Anyone driving your car yesterday?" he asked.

"Goodness, no. I don't trust this baby with anyone else. Not even my husband."

Riley wasn't sure he believed her. "What business do you have here in Lincolnville, Ms. Jameson?"

"I just pulled off the highway after shopping in New York. I'm headed to Atlanta, but thought I'd stop at your local grocery to grab a couple of things."

"Lincolnville's not exactly the direct route from New York." Riley caught the smell of her expensive perfume.

"I stopped off and saw a friend in Chattanooga." She pulled her sunglasses off and stared up at him with grey eyes. "Did I do something wrong?"

"No. I was just checking." Riley handed her back the license. "Here. Sorry to have delayed you."

"That's quite all right. I sure hope you catch your man." She pressed the button to roll her window up and drove onto the highway.

Riley walked back to his car. What were the chances of two strangers driving a Lexus in a small town like Lincolnville? He pulled out his cell and dialed BJ's number.

"Hello." BJ sounded out of breath.

"Are you all right?"

"Yes, I am. You know I'm healthy as a horse. I was in the back room and left my phone up front, so I had to rush to get it." There was a pause. "So, what can I do for you?"

"I need Calley's number. I'm assuming you have it."

"Hah! I knew you liked that girl."

Riley shook his head. "It has nothing to do with that. She'd asked me to check into something, and I've got information for her."

"Nothing serious, I hope." Her concern for Calley was evident.

"Not that I'm aware of."

Riley dreaded dialing the number. Would Calley assume his call was more than just professional? It didn't matter. He had to let her know about the Lexus.

"Hello." Music blared in the background when she answered.

"Calley, it's Riley." The noise lowered. "I just wanted to let you know I stopped a woman in a black Lexus. Does the name Fifi Jameson mean anything to you?"

Hesitation came over the line. "No. Never heard of her." Her voice quivered.

"She and her husband, a lawyer, live in Atlanta."

"I'm sorry. Doesn't ring a bell. We'll I'll let you go. I know you have other things to do. Thanks anyway and goodbye." She clicked off the line.

Riley stared at the phone. She wasn't a very good liar. She knew who this woman was, and it unnerved her. What could Calley be mixed up in? Riley turned toward the sky. He'd done what he could. It was God's job now to keep her safe.

CALLEY DROVE INTO THE gallery lot and parked the car. What if Fifi Jameson continued to follow her? The thought of being harassed in every store she visited unnerved her. Calley pulled out her cell phone.

When the receptionist answered, Calley said, "Peter Jameson, please."

"May I ask who's calling, please?"

"Calley Regan."

Boring elevator music played while Calley waited on hold. With as much as they make, you would think they could afford better music.

"I'm sorry," the receptionist said, returning to the line. "He's unavailable right now. Would you like to leave a message with me or on his voice-mail?"

Anger burned in Calley. How dare he not take her calls. "I'll just leave one with you. You can tell him how little I appreciated his wife accosting me in the store today. After all, I'm not the one who kept their marriage a secret." She paused. "Do you have all that?"

"Yes." The girl choked on the word.

"Thank you for all your help. Have a good day."

She flew out of the driver's seat and opened the door behind hers. She tugged out one of Sheryl's paintings and carried it inside.

"Hey there, Miss Pregnant Lady. You shouldn't be carrying anything heavy in your condition." Eva took the art from Calley's hands. "Do you have any more out there?"

"Two other pieces."

Eva headed outside and carried in both. "These are wonderful. That girl is an amazing artist."

"There's a list of buyers who are looking for more art by Sheryl. I'll call them if you'd like me to."

"There's plenty of time for that." Eva walked from the back storeroom. "Tell me about the shower. Better yet, show me the pictures I'm sure you have on your phone. I'll make up the story as I go."

Calley grinned and handed over her phone.

"Okay, this must be the woman who owned the home you stayed in. She looks ornery. Probably has some bodies buried under that house." Eva let out a low whistle. "I don't know who this is, but I'd sure like to." She spun the phone toward Calley.

"He's the sheriff. His name's Riley. BJ's his aunt." Calley pulled up her chair behind her desk. "He gave me a ticket for speeding."

"He is one hot babe." Eva clicked some more. "Sheryl. Your cousin. Birds, flowers, whatever. How come you don't have more of the good-looking cowboy?"

"I didn't know you'd want an album of him."

"Who wouldn't?" Eva handed back the phone to Calley, then sat in a chair opposite her. "Anything interesting happen?"

Calley shrugged. "Let's see. My mother shot daggers when my pregnancy was unexpectedly announced. And Peter's wife cornered me in the local super-market."

"What? His wife?" Eva leaned forward, her elbows on her legs. "What was she doing there?"

"I think she followed me. In fact, it was her across the street the other day. She's apparently been spying on me."

"What a nut. What happened?"

"Nothing much. Basically, she told me to leave her husband alone." Calley figured she was also the woman who'd let the air out of her tires, but she wouldn't accuse her without knowing for sure.

"What'd you do?"

"I hid in the store until I was sure she wasn't following me."

"Too bad. You should have told her to get her old man neutered. I'm sure you weren't the first, and you won't be his last." Eva stood. "And there's little doubt she knows all about them."

Eva was probably right. Did Calley know how to pick 'em or what?

"Oh, don't look so down. So, he turned out to be a creep. At least one thing good came out of it."

Calley touched her belly. "Peter's wife apparently doesn't know about the baby because she didn't mention it. I can't imagine what she'd do if she ever found out."

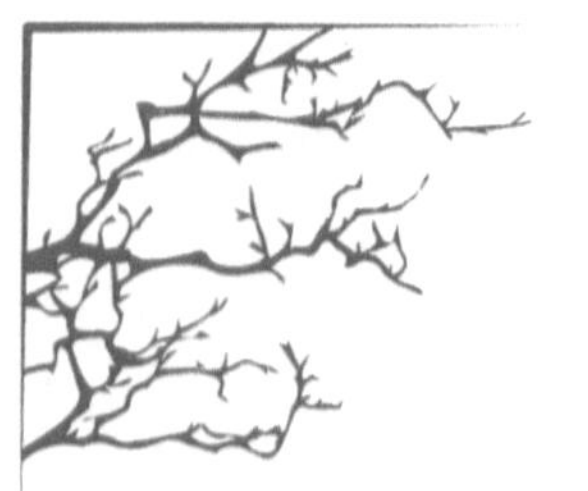

6

Riley took a seat at Fred's Diner. Greasy French fry aroma filled the air. It had been a long night with several burglaries, and he'd missed breakfast. It was already lunchtime. He glanced outside to the parking spot where Calley had pulled into months before. Why did he miss her so? She was nothing like the women who usually attracted him. Nothing like Beth, who had been blonde and serious.

"Sheriff, what can I get you?" Dolly walked up. She slid the pencil from her hair, which was pulled up on the back of her head.

"Bacon cheeseburger."

"All the way?"

"No onions."

"One day I'm going to ask you that, and you're going to surprise me by just saying yes, keep those onions on that burger." She laughed and walked off.

"One day." He knew it wouldn't happen because he was too predictable. You knew when he'd walk through the door at the office each morning unless he got a call. Never a vacation. He worked six days a week, at least ten hours a day. The sun shone through the letters advertising the daily special on the window. He used to enjoy fishing. Now, he spent all his days working. So why did he miss having fun now?

"Riley, is that you?"

He recognized the voice immediately. "Hello, Marylou."

"Mind if I sit while I wait for my order?" She didn't wait for a response. Instead, she slid on down on the opposite side of him in the

46

booth. "I heard Lydia's looking for a new singer for her wedding. What happened to that Calley girl?"

"You'd have to ask Lydia." Riley wasn't about to spread any gossip about anyone in his town.

Marylou nodded. "I just thought with how close you looked, you might know. Have you talked to her since she left?"

"We talk on the phone every once in a while."

Marylou's brow narrowed, and she frowned. As much as Riley hated to hurt her, he wasn't going to her know there was nothing between him and Calley. It would only get her hopes up.

"Here's your food." Dolly brought a bag and placed it in front of Marylou.

"Gotta get back to work." Marylou scooted out of the booth and stood. "See you soon."

"See ya." Riley returned his stare to the parking lot and his memory of his and Calley's first meeting.

"Riley, are you all right?" Dolly poured coffee into his cup.

"Fine. Why do you ask?"

"You seem preoccupied. I thought maybe something happened that I hadn't heard about."

"No, nothing." He took a sip from the cup. The heat floated down his system. He hadn't lied. There was nothing wrong. He wasn't about to tell her that except for a few phone calls, the most enjoyable woman he'd met in a long time had exited his life. And months later, she was still all he could think about.

CALLEY TOOK A SIP OF the cold water. She again tried to push slot A into hole E. It wasn't working. Why didn't it fit? Her patience waned. They'd been trying to get the crib together since they closed the gallery. She tossed the board aside onto the light blue carpet of her master suite in the two-bedroom apartment.

"Calm down there, girl," Eva said. "We'll get it figured out."

"I don't understand why it doesn't work."

It had been over two months since she'd left Lincolnville. She'd caught herself on more than one occasion, glancing at the picture of Riley still on her phone. It was hard for her to focus. For some reason, he stood at the forefront of her mind.

She never heard from Peter, and his wife appeared to not be following her anymore. She tried to shove the two pieces together again. It did no good.

"I just don't know how it fits." Calley let out a growl. "Maybe if they used one language, they'd have room to put pictures."

Eva sat across from her and giggled. "That's why I have a husband to do that type of nonsense for me. The pieces never seem to fit."

Calley's phone rang.

"I may have to ask your husband to put this together for us. A lopsided cradle just isn't a good thing." Calley leaned over and picked up her phone. She checked the display window to see who was calling before she answered. "Hello, BJ."

"Why hi there, darling." BJ's familiar voice sounded over the line. They'd spoken almost every other week since Calley left. "And how are you doing tonight?"

"Eva and I are trying to put together a cradle, and it's not going too well." She sighed. It was about time for BJ to be putting dinner on the table. Calley could still taste the wonderful roast from her first night there. And the gravy. Calley's never had such good meaty flavor. Her stomach growled.

"How's that friend of yours?" BJ interrupted Calley's thoughts.

"She's looking hungry," Calley said. Even if Eva wasn't, Calley now was.

"I'm always hungry." Eva yelled loud enough to cause BJ to laugh.

Calley tried one last time to fit the pieces together. "How's everything there in Lincolnville? Everyone excited about the big wedding?" It had taken her a couple of weeks to convince Lydia she wouldn't be available to sing. As much as Calley wished she could be there, she knew it was better if she didn't attend. She was grateful when Lydia finally consented and found someone else.

"I think Sheryl's having the time of her life with all the wedding preparations."

"I'll bet. You know how she likes to be in the thick of things." Calley swallowed down her emotions. She'd hated missing the wedding. "And what's new with you?"

"Oh, there's never anything new with me. You're the one with all the excitement. I sure wish you were up here. I'd love to be helping you with all this baby stuff." BJ's voice held longing to it. She had no children of her own, and Riley didn't seem set to have a family anytime soon.

"Unfortunately, my belly is sticking out pretty good now." Calley subconsciously touched her midsection. Once the baby was born, she might feel different about revisiting Lincolnville, but right now she didn't want the stares. "I swear to you this kid's lying horizontal instead of in a fetal position."

BJ laughed out loud. "I'm assuming most pregnant women feel that way."

"I actually found a stretch mark the other day. I thought I was going to die."

"From what I've heard, you'll probably get one or two more."

"That's not helping any."

"Yeah, eating all those pickles and ice cream I keep bringing over doesn't help either," Eva yelled as she spread the instructions out in front of her.

Calley used the railing from her four-poster bed to pull herself up from the floor. She walked over to the baby lotion on the dresser and took in a whiff. She kept hoping the aroma would make her feel more like a mother. Maybe mother's intuition didn't kick in until after the baby was born.

"I'm glad you've got someone there with you," BJ said. "Oops, the gravy's boiling. Talk to Riley for a moment. I have to add more cornstarch." Calley realized weeks ago BJ made a practice of calling when Riley was home for supper. It was a habit Calley had yet to discourage. His voice made her feel more at ease, like maybe the world wasn't ashamed of her.

"Hello."

His deep voice caused her heart to race. How could she be attracted to this man? Sure, he was handsome, also a good worker, and kind, but professional men were more her type. Men like Peter. Riley was the first man she'd taken a strong notice to who was a jeans-and t-shirt type of guy.

"Hey. How's it been going?" She hoped her voice didn't give away the rapid beating of her pulse.

"Same old thing."

"Giving tickets out to more pregnant women, huh?" Calley teased.

"Only if they're breaking the law." There was a lull in the conversation. "Are you coming to the wedding in a couple of weeks?"

Eva scooted over and placed her ear against the phone and listened. She moved a foot or two away and whispered, "Let me guess, the good-looking sheriff."

Calley nodded, and her cheeks burned. "I don't think so," she said into the phone. As much as she wanted to see Lydia married and happy, everyone would know her secret. The fact her mother would be there gave her even more pause. Allison had called and warned her Uncle Joe would attend as a guest of their mother. Another reason not to go.

"Everyone will find out eventually. Hiding isn't going to help." Did Calley catch a hint of disappointment in his voice?

"Right now, I'm not ready to face the stares." She got up and walked to the kitchen. She glanced into the refrigerator, then the freezer. A blast of cool air sent shivers over her arm. "I received enough of those from my own mother in just one visit." A knock sounded. "Can you hold on a second? Someone's at the door."

"I'll get it." Eva rushed over and looked out the peephole. "It's a man in a brown uniform. You know what that means. A present."

Eva clicked the deadbolt and turned the knob. The door flew open, and Eva fell to the floor. Calley screamed when she saw the knife in the man's hand.

A SCREAM OVER THE PHONE shocked Riley. A shuffle sounded on the other end of the line.

"Calley! Calley!" Riley yelled into the phone, but she didn't answer.

"What's wrong?" BJ rushed in from the kitchen, concern carried in her eyes.

Riley jumped when a gunshot sounded. "Calley!"

He handed the phone to BJ. "Stay on the line. I'll get someone over there." He grabbed his cell and his car keys off the counter by the door.

"Wait, here's her address." BJ shoved a piece of paper at him.

Riley raced out the door. "Hello. Sylvi, get me someone in the Atlanta Police Department. It's an emergency."

Riley rushed out to his car. He couldn't be sure if his lack of breath came from the hot air or his fear of what happened. *God, please don't let her or the baby be hurt.* He slammed down into the seat and shoved the key into the ignition. His tires kicked up dirt as he sped down the gravel driveway toward the main road. He shouldn't have let her out of his sight. How could he protect her when she wasn't near?

"Riley." Silvi returned to the line. "I have Officer Reynolds with the APD on the line with us."

"Reynolds, this is Sheriff Riley Owens of Lincolnville, Georgia. I was just speaking to someone on the phone when I heard a gunshot. You need to get over there. And Reynolds, send an ambulance. She's about seven months pregnant." After he gave the address to the officer, he tossed his phone down on the passenger seat.

Riley gripped the steering wheel as he drove down Plaskett. He was doing ninety when he hit I-75, siren squealing and lights on, though he would have no jurisdiction once he left his county. His heart throbbed so loud he heard it in his ears.

Please don't let me have failed this time.

"EVA, YOU'RE GOING TO be okay." Calley rocked her friend in her arms. Blood covered Eva's once white blouse. "Hold on! Hold on!"

"I'm sorry." Eva sputtered when she spoke. "I haven't planned the shower yet."

"It's all right. You don't have to do anything but stay with me." Tears flowed from Calley's eyes. She pulled her friend tighter. The smell of Eva's hairspray drifted into her. "Please don't go."

The .38 Calley had bought when she returned from Lincolnville was still in her trembling right hand. Did she hit him? She couldn't recall. Gun-powder drifted into her sinuses.

Eva stared up at her. "You're going to be okay. Take care of that bab..." She jerked then her eyes closed.

"No! No. Please. No." Calley sobbed into her friend's hair.

A knock startled her.

"Ms. Regan?"

She didn't speak. She raised the weapon. If he walked through the door, she'd put a hole in him so big they'd never fill it.

"Ms. Regan, it's the police."

Calley didn't trust him. The man with the knife had dressed in a brown delivery uniform.

The door moved. She raised the gun level with her right eye. Her bloody hand shook. "I've got a gun. Show me your badge." She continued to cradle Eva with her left arm.

A hand holding a badge snuck through the door. "Riley Owens, the sheriff of Lincolnville called us."

The breath she'd been holding released. "Come in. Please hurry." She sobbed out the words. Two officers entered, one clean-shaven, the other had a mustache. The officer with the mustache rushed to her. The name on his shirt read R.J. Petri.

"Please help her," Calley cried.

He placed two fingers on the side of Eva's neck, looked up at his partner, and shook his head.

"No. No. No." Calley pulled Eva even tighter.

Petri peeled Calley's arms from around Eva and forced her up from the floor. He walked her to the doorway. "Are you all right?"

"I'm pregnant."

"We know. Paramedics are on the way. What happened?"

"I-I don't know." She tried to think back. "Someone kicked in my door. He had a knife. He stabbed..." She looked over at Eva. Next to her body was the gun. Calley wasn't sure when she'd released it.

The clean-shaven officer picked up the weapon and sniffed it. "It's been fired."

Petri nodded and pulled Calley into the hallway. "Where did you get the gun?"

"What?" She looked down at her hands soaked with her friend's blood. "It was in my pocket. I shot at him."

"Do you know who did this?"

She wiped her sleeve across her nose and shook her head.

The officer continued to hold her arms above the elbow and stare into her eyes. "Did you hit him?"

"N-no." Her lip trembled. Lightheadedness rushed in, and her knees buckled. Petri guided her to the floor.

Two paramedics rushed off the elevator, rolling a gurney. "What have we got?"

"This one's pregnant and needs medical evaluation." He used his head to point at Calley. "The other's inside with my partner." He shook his head.

"Stop that." Tears continued down Calley's cheeks. "Don't shake your head. It makes her..."

Petri moved aside and let the paramedic take over. He listened to Calley's heart. Then he took her blood pressure. "Let's get you up on this." He helped Calley onto the gurney.

Calley stared at the ceiling on the way out. Everything blurred in her vision. Every part of her body had grown numb until her heart burned. She reached up and touched the arm of the paramedic who sat in the back with her. Fear engulfed her. How could she make him understand?

"I know. Don't talk." He patted her hand.

Pain seared through her left side. *Please God, if you really do care for me, prove it just once in my awful life. Don't take my child.* She worked to keep her eyes opened. She tried to focus, but everything faded and went to black.

IT TOOK RILEY HALF the time it should have to get to Atlanta. Good thing for that sheriff's emblem on his car. His hands hurt from having gripped the steering wheel the entire drive over. He pulled off

I-75 and slowed for traffic. He glanced around at the skyline of downtown. It had been a long time since he'd been in Atlanta. Funny. He didn't miss it at all. His phone rang, and he reached over to get it.

"Riley Owens."

"Sheriff, this is Officer Reynolds." His voice was matter of fact with a true cop tone.

"What've we got?" He was almost afraid to ask, but he had to know.

"They're taking one victim to the hospital. The other was DOA."

Riley's stomach bounced into his throat. "Which one?" He wasn't sure whether his voice squeaked when he spoke.

"A Miss Eva Martinez."

Riley hated himself instantly for the relief he felt. "And Ms. Regan?"

"They're taking her to the Atlanta Medical Center. She was pretty hysterical when we arrived. She collapsed. The officers thought she was fine at first, but she passed out in the ambulance. Right now she's listed as serious but stable. We don't know if it's a problem with her or the baby. I'll call you if I find out more."

"Thanks for the update." Riley knew Atlanta Medical was a level 1 trauma center. That's where they took those that might not make it. His heart pounded in his chest. He pressed his foot all the way down on the accelerator.

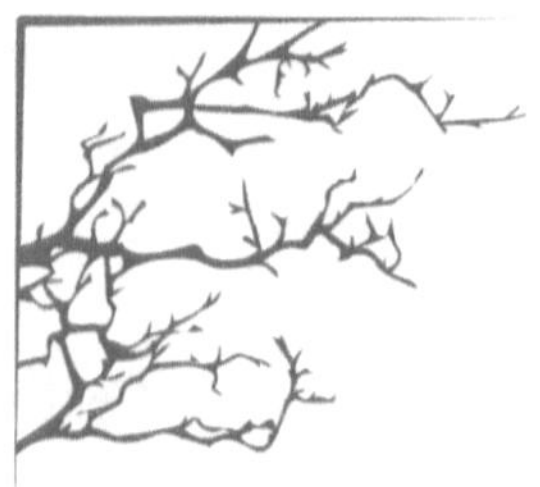

7

Riley sat in the lot of Atlanta Medical on Parkway Drive. The August sun made the car hot, even with the air cranked up. The back of his shirt stuck to his skin. A trickle of sweat slid from his forehead to his chin. He couldn't force himself to get out of the car. What if she died, too? Could he take another loss?

He knew what he needed to do. Calley wouldn't like it, but a member of her family should be here with her. Her mother wasn't what she needed. She needed people who cared for her. BJ was one, Lydia the other. He dialed Matthew's number.

"Hello best man of mine." Matthew had yet to take the smile off his face since Lydia agreed to marry him. His happiness even showed in the tone of his voice.

"Matthew." Riley's voice was solemn.

"Hey, what's wrong? You aren't calling to tell me you're not cancel—"

"Matthew, it's about Calley Regan."

Silence came over the line. Matthew finally said, "What happened?"

"Someone broke into her place. Her friend was killed, and she's at the hospital. They tell me it's bad." Riley wiped a tear sliding along his jawline. "Can you get BJ and drive her to Atlanta?"

"We're on the way."

He knew Matthew would also bring Lydia. Riley only hoped Calley and the baby made it. Not that she'd be happy once she saw her cousin. A plan formed in his mind, and Lydia could be beneficial in bringing it to fruition.

CALLEY WATCHED THE blip on the machine as it took her heartbeat. Her whole body ached, inside and out. A wrap surrounding her finger constantly guarded her blood oxygen levels. A mild heart attack. She was too young to have a heart attack. The doctor had explained that hypertension added pressure on the artery walls leading into the heart. That's why she had the attack. The pregnancy gave her added stress. But Calley knew watching Eva die pushed her over the edge.

A chill went to her bones. No matter how hard she tried, she couldn't get warm. She'd probably never feel warm again.

"I'm not doing a very good job of protecting you. Am I?" She placed her hand on her belly. "Maybe I should have stuck to the original plan and gotten lost, then Eva wouldn't..." Tears gathered in her eyes. She had no proof the guy was after her, but it did little to sway her guilt.

Calley jumped when a nurse entered the room.

"It's all right." The older woman talked as she picked up the chart from the end of the bed. "You're safe here. You've got a good-looking cop standing outside your door." She walked over and looked at the monitors. "How are you feeling?"

"Okay, I guess." Calley tucked her hands beneath the blanket so the nurse couldn't see them tremble.

"Everything looks pretty good. The technician will be up in a few minutes to do the sonogram. We just need to check to see on the baby."

Calley nodded. She rubbed her arms up and down. A sob caught in her throat when she saw the blood beneath her fingernails. The nurse came around and stood on the side of the bed. She checked Calley's pulse and temperature and a few other things.

"I heard you lost a friend." The nurse patted her hand. "I'm sorry. Is there someone you want me to call? Your mother? The baby's father?"

Calley shook her head and whispered, "There's nobody out there who cares about us anymore."

RILEY SPED TO THE NURSES' station on the first floor. He still wore his badge and holster, yet there was no shock on the women's faces. The trauma center saw its share of weapons. Not just from law enforcement.

"I understand they brought Calley Regan here." He hoped his voice didn't quiver as bad as his insides.

A nurse typed on the keyboard in front of her. "She's in room three, down the hall to your right."

The further into the hospital Riley rushed, the more the aroma of antiseptic attacked him. A woman's voice sounded on the intercom overhead. He rounded the corner in what felt like a run with the way his heart raced. His boots pounded on the tile floor.

Room three was on the right. An officer stood guard outside. The man who murdered Calley's friend must still be at large. He recognized the officer from a drug case they'd worked on just prior to him leaving for Lincolnville.

"John, how are you?" Riley extended his hand. He hadn't seen John Stevens in over four years.

"I'm doing well. This lady inside a friend of yours?" There was a glint in John's eyes.

"I know her. Do you know what happened?"

"Nothing official. Just what the guys told me. Someone kicked in her door and went after her friend. She had a gun and actually got a couple shots off. One hit the guy. Dots of blood were found on the floor heading out and down the hallway to the staircase. Probably wasn't serious, but it was enough to stop him from finishing Ms. Regan off."

"I was told she passed out in the ambulance. Have you heard about her condition?" He wanted to be prepared before he walked in.

"She seems to be doing fine. Something about her blood pressure, I think." John patted Riley's arm. "They're just running tests on her and the baby to make sure."

"I assume they haven't caught the guy or you wouldn't be here."

"Not yet. But I'll put the word out he went after a cop's family. That'll give some incentive up and down the ranks."

Riley nodded. He chose not to correct the man. Cops never liked people who messed with their loved ones. It left a bad taste in their mouths and makes them want the perpetrator that much more. Riley removed his cowboy hat. He touched the door and inhaled deep. The last thing he wanted Calley to see was the concern on his face. He crept through the door so as not to disturb her if she were sleeping. Instead, she stared out the nearby window. She jumped and turned when the door closed.

"Hey, Sheriff. You're a long way from home." Her voice was hoarse and weak. Her bottom lip quivered, and tears fell from her eyes.

"I was on the phone when it happened. Remember?" He walked over to the side of the bed. "BJ's on her way."

She wiped her tears with the back of the hand. "I'm sorry. I forgot about the call." She sniffled. "Is BJ all right?"

"Yeah. I'm sorry about your friend." He took hold of Calley's hand.

She pulled from his touch and covered her face with her hands as she sobbed. Riley sat beside her. He wrapped an arm around her and drew her into him. His heart ached at her pain. He didn't know how long he'd held on before she pushed herself away and reclined back on the bed.

"How's the baby?" He continued to sit next to her.

"I don't know for sure. They want to do a sonogram. But the way he's bouncing around in there, I think he's okay." Calley returned her stare back out the window. "They said they haven't got the guy who killed Eva yet."

Calley's tear-stained face broke Riley's heart.

"No. But don't worry. You're being guarded, and I'm not leaving here until *you* do." He squeezed her hand. "I have a feeling BJ will say the same." He wiped a tear that rolled down her cheek.

The door bounced opened, and a young woman with an ultrasound machine came in. "I understand we have us a kid to check on." The technician shoved the cart toward the bed. "I'd like to say I warmed the pad up, but that would be a lie."

Calley forced a smile.

"I'll wait outside." Riley turned to go.

"No. Please stay." Calley took hold of his arm. An anxious look came over her face. "Just in case. I don't want to be alone. Not with everything else."

Riley tossed his hat on a nearby chair and walked around to the other side of the bed. When the nurse placed the probe on Calley's stomach, she grabbed hold of Riley's hand. Warmth rushed through him at the softness of her fingers mingled with his.

"Well, looky there," the technician said. "We have us a head. Wow, this kid's got some long fingers, too. Must gonna be a piano player."

The clarity amazed Riley. He'd never seen anything so wonderful in his life. He glanced down at Calley. A tear ran from her eyes. He hoped it was a tear of relief.

"If I can tell, do you want to know the sex of the baby?" The technician continued to stare at the motion on the screen.

"Yes." Calley's grip on Riley's hand tightened.

"Well, what's this? I guess we're looking at a boy. Oh, now stop kicking me." The technician looked at Riley. "A macho man like you will be handing out cigars when you get home, huh?"

Riley didn't respond. Since Beth's death, his dreams of a family had died, too. But looking at this image of a baby made him long for one of his own.

"A boy," Calley said. "I'm having a boy. A son."

The tech continued to move the pad around the protruding belly. "He's an active little thing, isn't he?"

"Yeah. He's always moving."

"That's good. Maybe he'll get it out of his system before he comes." She wiped gel off Calley's stomach and placed the probes back on the portable machine. "I'll get this right to your doctor. And you two enjoy the rest of your day."

Calley's hand touched her stomach. "He looked healthy, didn't he?" She looked up at Riley with pleading eyes.

"Real healthy." He gave her a nod. "I'm not sure how you handle a kid kicking you like that. When do you sleep?"

"When he gives me a chance. Eva was always good about letting me rest." She turned her head away as a sob escaped. "Do you think they'll catch the guy?"

"I don't know." He felt the need to be honest with her. The truth would only ensure her safety. "Do you know who it might be or why he came in after you two?"

Calley shook her head.

Riley hated to see the frown on her face. He liked the fun Calley. The one who laughed and danced to music. He walked back to the other side of the bed, where he pulled up a chair. He didn't know how long he'd been there when a commotion outside the door drew his attention. When he glanced back at Calley, fear stood in her eyes and her breathing intensified. Riley stood and took hold of her hand. He gave her hand a quick squeeze and unsnapped his holster.

Angry voices sounded outside the room.

"I don't care who you are. I want in that room."

Riley immediately recognized BJ's voice. "It's BJ." He removed his hand from the weapon and patted Calley on the shoulder.

Calley gasped when the door burst opened, and BJ and Lydia ran in, followed by Pastor Matthew Winters.

CALLEY SWALLOWED HARD. There's no way she could hide the fact she was pregnant anymore. It's bad enough Lydia was standing over her with her mouth opened wide, but her soon-to-be preacher husband stood there as well.

"Are you all right?" BJ rushed up to the bed and shoved Riley over. She slid a hip on the edge of the mattress. "I'm so sorry about Eva, child."

Tears drove over Calley's lashes, and she sobbed. She was surprised by all the tears she still had left.

BJ cuddled her close. "There, there. It's going to be all right." She held Calley while she cried. "You'll get through this. In time, we'll remember Eva's sense of humor and her love for you." She released her hold and brushed the hair from Calley's face. Calley leaned back, and BJ took a tissue from the side table and wiped Calley's cheeks. "How's the baby?"

"I think he's okay." Tension rose in the pit of Calley's stomach when she glanced over BJ's shoulder and saw Lydia staring down at her.

"Why didn't you tell us you were pregnant?" Lydia patted the blanket covering Calley's leg.

"It didn't really seem like the right moment." Calley sucked in a breath and straightened up the best she could.

"Sheryl's going to be angry that I found out something before she did." Lydia moved Riley even further away and reached over and gave Lydia a kiss on her forehead.

Lydia's perfume wafted over Calley. She always smelled so good.

"This explains why you were always so pale and tired when you were in Lincolnville." Lydia grinned. She raised Calley's chin up. "You'll get through this. It'll take time, but you will. Especially once this baby is born. I'm sure it'll help you through the grief."

Calley was stunned. How could she be so wrong about everyone's reaction? Maybe they were just being nice because of Eva.

"You scared the dickens out of me." The caring in BJ's eyes made Calley feel warm inside. "I'm an old woman. Never do that to me again."

"I'm sorry."

"But you and the baby are fine?"

"I am. They just took a sonogram, but he looked healthy. Didn't he, Riley?" She didn't want to worry BJ by telling her about the heart attack.

"He sure did," Riley said.

"He. It's a boy?" BJ's smile widened.

"Yeah, I just found out."

"Well, isn't that something?" BJ pumped a fist in the air. "I should have known with the way he's been kicking you. I remember when Riley's mom was carrying him. You'd have thought he was a bucking bronco."

Riley lowered his face, and his cheeks reddened.

Matthew walked to the head of the bed. "I'm glad you're all right. If you ever need anyone to talk to about your friend, please give me a call."

Calley nodded. She didn't know what to say.

"And about this kid."

Calley leaned back and prepared for the worst. She was too weak to put up any fight. Hopefully BJ would tell him off for her.

Matthew took her hand. "When you come up with a name, let me know. I'll have to get ready for a baptism. That is, if you'll allow me the pleasure." He showed no condemnation or ill will for this pregnant unmarried woman. If these people were true Christians, then how could her mother claim to be one?

"I'd appreciate that." A tear fell from Calley's eye. How could a minister be this kind to someone who had sinned as badly as she had?

"What is going on in here?" The nurse's tone was harsh. "Some of you will have to leave. There's too many in here. Now. And don't think I won't call security just because you have badges."

"I'll take my man out," Lydia said. "We haven't had anything to eat, and I'm sure my husband-to-be is hungry."

Matthew patted his stomach. "Always."

"You all can wait outside." The nurse had her hands on her hips. "We're taking her upstairs in a few moments and putting her in a room. Once she gets settled, you can see her then."

BJ rose and faced the nurse, who was older than Calley, but younger than BJ. "Young lady, I'm sure you're just following rules, but I have no intention of leaving her. And no amount of your security forces are going to change that. If you don't like it, you just put in a call to your superior."

The nurse glanced down at Calley who nodded and mouthed the word *please*. She must have seen something in Calley's expression that showed she needed someone with her right now. "All right, *you* can stay, but the rest have to go."

"I'll wait outside." Riley followed Matthew and Lydia to the door.

Calley hated Riley having to leave. He not only gave her comfort, but she felt safer with him nearby.

As if reading her mind, he stopped, turned to Calley, and said, "I won't be far."

A little over an hour later, Calley was in a private room upstairs. Lydia and Matthew left for home with Lydia's promise that if Calley had to stay in the hospital for more than a night, she'd be back up.

Calley's eyes drooped. The chills had finally dissipated, and she drifted in and out of sleep.

BJ sat on the edge of the bed and used her fingers to brush Calley's hair from her forehead. "While they were bringing you up, Riley and I discussed it. We want you to come to Lincolnville and stay with us. It's not safe for you to go back home. Not with this man still out there."

Calley glanced over at Riley, who sat on the windowsill. He didn't say a word and held no real expression on his face, making it hard to tell if they discussed it, or if BJ just told him what was what.

"I'm thinking of just taking off and not telling anyone where I am," Calley said.

"That's not very safe." Riley stood and took a step toward the bed. "If we don't know where you are, how are we supposed to know whether this guy has gotten hold of you?"

Calley shrugged. She had thought no one would really care.

"I think you need to come to Lincolnville," BJ said. "This way, we can make sure you and the baby are taken care of until this guy is caught."

"I don't know if that's a good idea. When everyone finds out about the baby, they might make it hard for Lydia and Matthew. It's probably not proper Christian protocol to have an unwed mother in the family."

"Now stop that." BJ flicked Calley's chin with her forefinger. "Matthew and Lydia have been through worse, and there's no way she wouldn't want you there. Besides, now that I know it's a boy, I have some ideas for decorating a nursery." The gleam in her eye told Calley how much BJ wanted her to come with her.

Riley took another step toward the bed. "Besides you only have of couple of options. You can either go to Lincolnville, or I can have the Atlanta Police can put into protective custody."

"Since when did you have any say over my life?"

Riley leaned over the bed and stared into her eyes. "Since you got my aunt hooked on you." He stood upright. "I guess there is one other choice."

"What's that?" Calley rolled her eyes.

"I can take a leave of absence from work and disappear with you."

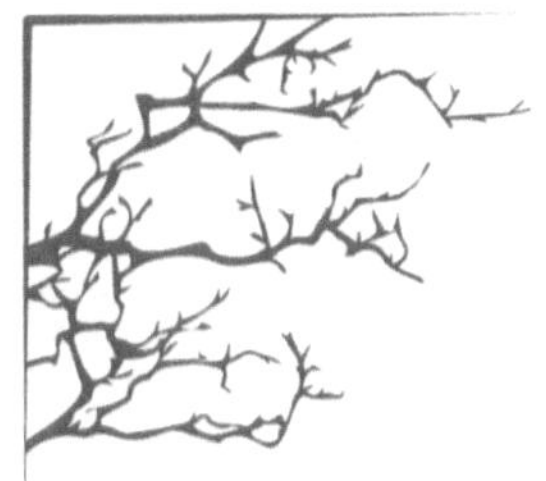

8

Riley glanced over at Calley as he drove. The way her jaw clenched, it made him wonder if she might chip a tooth. They had taken the necessities from her apartment, stayed long enough for Eva's private funeral, and then headed straight to Lincolnville.

The detective investigating the stabbing told Riley that this was the third home invasion in the area where Calley lived where women were attacked with a knife, neither killed. They were too fragile to describe their attacker. That left Calley.

If he came for her, Riley would be ready.

"You can sit there and sulk the whole time, or you can learn to adjust." He gripped the steering wheel. Why did she have to be so stubborn? "This is the best way I know to keep you safe until we catch this guy. You got too good a look at him to stay in Atlanta."

"I'm not sulking." She turned her head, so she faced the passenger-side window. "I just don't think this is a good idea. The guy might know Lincolnville is where I'd go."

"How could he unless you know him? And strangers stick out in a small town. It'll be easier to spot someone there than most other places."

"It'd just be safer for me to disappear."

"Then let's stop. I'll pack a few things and say goodbye to BJ before we take off."

"You're just trying to get out of doing the toast at the wedding." She crossed her arms over her chest, but her eyes twinkled, and the corners of her mouth curled up. "You want to go because you'd miss me if I wasn't around."

67

Riley shook his head. This woman drove him crazy. One moment she was mad, the next playing around. But in the long run, she was right.

"You can't admit it. Can you?" Calley said. "I've gotten under your skin." She leaned her head back on the seat and looked over at him.

"I'm just trying to keep my aunt from being hurt." He tried to keep focused on the road, but his attention wanted to center on her instead. His eyes constantly looked her way.

"You can say it's all BJ, but I know better." Almost as quick as it came, her smile faded, and she straightened. "Do you think it'll be safe for BJ with me around?"

"BJ might not look like much in the way of strength, but don't let her small stature fool you. She was born and raised a farm girl." He ran his hand through his hair. "She also knows how to handle a gun."

"It'll only be until the baby comes, anyway. Then you won't have to worry."

"Why's that?"

"I'm thinking of giving him up for adoption so this guy can never hurt him. I'm assuming he's after the baby to sell or something."

"What makes you think that?"

"It's all I have that's important."

"If so, then why come at you with a knife now if it's the baby he wants? He'd wait until it's safe to take him. There's no way the boy would have survived without you if taken now." Riley stretched his fingers out. He hadn't realized how tense his hands were. "This guy wanted your or Eva dead. And you claim to not know who why."

"I don't."

The hesitation in her voice caused him doubt.

She must have heard the skepticism in her own voice, because she added, "I know you don't believe me, but I don't care. I may be a whore, but I'm not a liar."

Riley jerked the car to the side of the road. "I don't ever want to hear that word again. You made a mistake. Everyone does. You need to stop listening to that mother of yours and realize you're worth ten of her."

"It's just hard when you're alone, and the only thing you hear is bad stuff about yourself." She stared down at her lap.

"You're alone because you distance yourself. A lot of people care about you. You just need to realize it." He took her chin in his hand and turned her face toward him. "Are you listening?"

"Yeah." Her voice broke as she spoke.

He wiped a tear straggling down her cheek. "And no matter what that pompous mother of yours says, you're a wonderful person. You have a great sense of humor, and you care about others. Or you wouldn't be worried about BJ or hurt by losing your friend."

Riley stared down at her. Her mouth looked so inviting. He stroked her cheek with his knuckles. His thumb ran over her lips. Her mouth opened slightly. She leaned into his touch.

He shook his head. If they didn't get back on the road, he'd do something they both might regret. He pulled the car back onto the interstate. Focus, focus, focus. He had to take his focus off Calley and put it where it should be.

"Wow." Calley's voice sounded light. "I think that's the most you've ever said to me at one time."

Riley bit his tongue to keep from smiling. She was right. In a short period, she'd gotten under his skin. More than that, she'd gotten into his heart.

CALLEY THOUGHT ABOUT what had just happened. She thought he was going to kiss her, but then stopped. She was sure of it.

Would she have allowed it? She ran a hand over her lips, glanced over at Riley, who stared out at the road. Little doubt she would have returned the kiss. There was only one explanation.

Hormones.

Trees passed by in a blur as the car sped down the interstate. How could Riley keep BJ safe with a killer on the hunt? And why did someone want her dead? She'd never hurt anyone bad enough to cause this type of hatred. It made no sense.

With the world today, it could just be some psycho she'd cut off in traffic, and he wanted her to pay for it.

The blue sky did nothing to help her mood. *God, help me get through this.* She wished she had the faith her family did. You can't feel alone with God on your side. It'd been a long time since she felt Him inside her heart. Not since before that day in the back room of the garage with Uncle Joe. Calley rubbed her arms up and down to get the chill out. She needed God now more than ever before. Unfortunately, He'd turned his back on her.

"Are you cold?" Riley's voice startled her.

"A bit."

He turned down the air. "Better?"

She nodded. "Oof." Calley fidgeted in the seat. "That was a good one."

"What's wrong?" Concern carried in Riley's voice.

"The kid just gave me a good wallop." She glanced at Riley, whose brow creased. "Don't worry. I'm not going into labor. After what I did to your boots, I'd hate to ruin your car as well."

He glanced over at her with a scowl.

"Oh, come on, it was a joke." She laughed. "You really need to loosen up. It would just be another story to tell your grandkids. A crazy woman having a kid in your car."

He stared straight ahead, but she saw his lips curve upward. Why did he try so hard not to smile? It would probably look good on him. Not that he didn't look good, anyway.

Stop that! Her hormones must really be out of control.

Riley slowed the car as they pulled off the highway into Lincolnville. Calley glanced at the houses on the way to Riley's. Most were large, two-story brick homes with perfectly manicured lawns.

When they passed the church, her stomach jumped. Sweat covered her palms. Could Lydia and Matthew face any scrutiny that would occur because of her? She hated the thought of messing up their lives because of her mistake.

Riley slowed the car and pulled off the road to a tree-lined gravel driveway. After rounding a curve, they came to a clearing leading up to the white L-shaped home. A multi-colored banner draped across the front porch. Green and yellow balloons hung on each side. The sign read WELCOME HOME.

A tear formed in her eye. It felt little like home to Calley, but she wouldn't say anything and take the chance on BJ finding out. Calley wouldn't hurt BJ's feelings for the world. "I see BJ's been busy." Her words were barely audible.

"She has." Riley got out of the car and walked to the trunk, where he pulled out Calley's two suitcases, then placed them on the ground. He took out the guitar and leaned it against the back passenger side door. "Can you get the guitar?"

Calley paused, looked toward the front porch and said, "Are you okay with this?" Riley stared up at the banner. "I know you're not much for pomp and circumstance," she added.

"I'm not thrilled with the announcement, and balloons aren't my thing either. But then again, you don't have a problem with the limelight, and BJ will do what BJ wants to do. It doesn't really matter how anyone feels about it."

Her heart sank. She couldn't tell if he wanted her here. Maybe it was really all for BJ. "I'm sorry."

"Not your fault. I suggest we get inside. I'm sure there's more."

Calley grabbed the guitar case and followed Riley in. BJ rushed out from the kitchen.

"Welcome. How are you holding up?" She gave Calley a hug and took the case from her hand.

"I'm fine. Thanks for the flowers for Eva's service. That was nice of you."

"I never did more than talk to the woman on the phone, but from what I got to know of her, I liked very much. Besides, any friend of yours has to be a wonderful person." BJ wrapped her hand around Calley's arm. "Now I've done some decorating. Not much, just a start. I didn't want to get carried away without your input."

Calley glanced around the living-room and kitchen area. She saw nothing new.

"Come on." BJ's grin told Calley something was up. Riley stood in the doorway of Calley's room after taking her bags inside. BJ handed him off the guitar. He headed back inside the room with the case.

BJ walked Calley into the second bedroom, the one where Allison had stayed. They'd repainted it from beige to a light blue color, and white clouds floated across the wall. A white tree painted in the corner had white branches reaching to the ceiling. The sun surrounded by a golden halo decorated the opposite wall. A painting of Jesus overlooking a small child hung to the right.

"I wasn't sure of the color," BJ said. "If you don't like it, we can change it. We still need a crib, changing table, and, of course, toys."

"Like it. I love it." In one corner was a white rocking chair with a blue pad that sat in the corner. "You did this for me?"

BJ again hugged her. A lump crawled into Calley's throat. She couldn't recall the last time anyone went to this type of trouble for her.

"Not just me. Sheryl did the clouds and the tree in the corner. And of course, the painting. I'm not sure who's more excited about this baby of yours. Her, or me." BJ walked to the rocking chair. "And this is from Lydia." She opened the seafoam green quilt folded on the chair. Giraffes, a tiger, and other baby animals covered the bedspread.

The gift took Calley's breath away. "This is so beautiful. I can't believe you all did this."

"Would you like this in your room or in here for now?" Riley spoke behind her.

She spun around, and her hand went to her heart. Riley stood beside the cradle she and Eva had tried to put together. It was no longer lopsided. Calley's lips trembled.

"Riley brought it here and finished putting it together," BJ said. "He added a special touch."

He'd attached a small gold plaque to the front of the rich brown wood. Calley bent to read it. "In Loving Memory of Eva Martinez". A sob caught in her throat.

"Calley, are you all right?" BJ placed her hands above Calley's elbows from behind her. "This must be too much for her. I just get carried away sometimes. Maybe you should lie down."

"No, I'm fine. I'm fine." She patted BJ's hand. "It's just so wonderful. It's all so very wonderful." She spun around, taking in all the kindness from her friends. For the first time in her life, Calley felt loved.

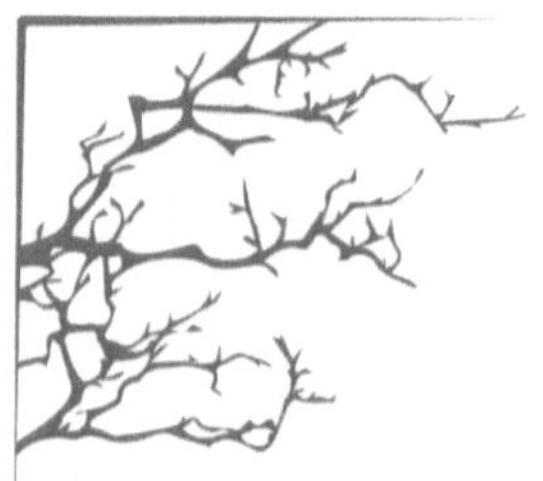

9

Riley stared out the glass patio doors. Calley sat on the picnic bench in the backyard, her guitar slung over one shoulder as she played and sang. It didn't matter that he didn't recognize the song. He really enjoyed her voice. She'd been there for a week now, and the police were no closer to finding out who killed Eva. He contemplated making her come inside, but he couldn't keep her hostage. It wouldn't be fair to someone who enjoyed being outdoors. Besides, he had officers driving past and keeping an extra eye out for any strangers. No one had seen anyone new around town.

"She's good. Isn't she?" BJ spoke over Riley's shoulder.

"Yes, she is."

"Why is it you allowed her to move in here?" BJ walked into the kitchen and pulled a jug of sweet tea from the refrigerator.

He didn't respond.

"Oh, you say it's because some guy might try to come after her," BJ said. "But there's more to it than that. When Lydia was in danger last year, you didn't move her in. Least not that I heard."

Riley turned away from the sliding glass doors. "This is different."

"How so?"

Irritation rose inside him. "It just is."

"You don't need to worry so much about her and the baby," BJ said. "I've got my best prayer warriors praying over her."

"It doesn't matter who's praying." His voice trailed off. "Not if it's God's will to take her."

BJ walked up to Riley and placed a hand on the side of his cheek. "You've lost a lot in your lifetime. Your parents, someone you wanted

74

to marry, and a brother roaming around out there doing Lord knows what. But it doesn't mean she's going to leave, too."

"I don't know what you're talking about."

Riley turned and walked into his room. BJ followed.

"You've got a look in your eye when you watch Calley. One I haven't seen in a long time. You like her. A lot. The fact she's got a child coming doesn't seem to bother you." BJ placed a finger on her chin. "In fact, I think that makes her even more appealing to a man like you."

"What type of man is that?" He wasn't too sure he wanted to hear the answer.

"A man who's been so lonely he's turned inside himself." Sadness reigned in BJ's tone. "A man who's been looking for someone special to take away that hurt he's felt for a long time."

"I need to get to work." Riley placed his holster around his shoulder. He didn't want to talk about his feelings for Calley or anyone else, for that matter. "Calley's here to be safe, nothing more. And when they find out killed Eva, she'll be on her way home."

"I'm not too sure about that." BJ followed Riley to the front door. A glimmer danced in her eyes. "Because that girl's got the same glint in her eye when she looks at you."

Riley stormed out to his car. BJ had Calley all set with a new doctor, determined not to let her go back to Atlanta. Had Calley really listened when he told her BJ got what BJ wanted? It didn't really matter. What did his aunt know about his feelings for Calley, anyway? Or Calley's feelings for him? He was too serious for someone like her. Besides, she needed a father for that baby. One who would have time to teach him to fish and play baseball, not a workaholic.

He sped off to the station. No matter how busy he kept himself, he couldn't erase BJ's words as thoughts of teaching Calley's son to throw a football played in his mind.

CALLEY SAT UNDER THE large oak tree. The blanket flowers in the garden with their bright yellow and rich red colors struck a nice contrast to the green of the grass. She'd never had much of a green thumb. Maybe BJ could teach her what plants would be easy to keep.

She strummed a few more chords on the acoustic guitar. The music soothed. She hadn't slept well in days. Nightmares of the man stabbing Eva invaded her dreams.

The sliding glass door opened behind her.

"Would you like something to eat?" BJ placed a hand on Calley's shoulder as she stood over her. "I could fix you a bagel and some yogurt. Or if you'd rather peanut butter on toast with pickles."

"Ugh. That doesn't sound good even to me. I think I'll take the bagel. But I can fix it. You don't have to wait on me."

"I enjoy it. You just stay out here in the fresh air. I'll bring us both one to enjoy outside."

Calley appreciated how BJ wanted to take care of her. That's the way a mother should be. Kind and caring. Her phone vibrated on the table. No name was listed on the caller I.D., and Calley didn't recognize the number.

"Hello."

"Calley. It's me." Allison whispered into the phone.

"Hi, Allison. Where are you calling from? I didn't recognize the number."

"I got a new phone. Mom had too much access to the prior bill and would scrutinize all my calls." She then added, "She wasn't happy about it, but I told her I was an adult and needed my privacy."

"Good for you."

"Lydia called and told us what happened. We were calling to check up on you."

Calley gave a laugh. There was no "we" calling to check up. Only Allison. "I'm okay. Still a bit scared, but I'm in Lincolnville for a while."

"But you're all right."

"Yes."

"And the baby?"

"He's okay, too."

"He? It's a boy." Allison's tone grew louder. "That's wonderful."

"Who are you talking to?" A harsh voice murmured in the background.

"Calley. She's okay, Mom."

"Of course, she is. She's always all right. No matter what type of trouble she gets herself into. Bet it was one of them boyfriends she's messing with. Always..." Her mother's voice faded.

"I need to go." Allison's voice lowered.

"I know." Calley inhaled deeply. "Allison, thanks for calling."

"Keep me posted."

"I will." Calley leaned forward with her elbows on the table. Allison had always tried to play the go-between in the family. Standing up for Calley and trying to keep her parents from getting mad. She'd make a wonderful aunt. It's too bad her mother would never be a loving grandmother.

RILEY HAD HEARD NO news from Atlanta. Even if there was nothing new, he should have at least gotten a phone call telling him so. His gut told him something was up.

He'd been smart enough to get John Stevens' number while he watched over Calley at the hospital. Maybe he'd at least know why there's been no information.

"Hello."

"John. It's Riley Owens."

"Riley. How are you and that lovely woman of yours?"

Riley again chose not to correct him on his misinformation. "She's doing very well. Thanks for asking. I called to see if you'd heard anything new on the case. I'm no longer in the loop up there, and nothing's come this way."

There was a pause. "Hold on a moment." Riley listened to what sounded like John walking. "You didn't get this from me, but prints from the wall across from the door, where they think he leaned on, came back from AFIS. The guy's name is Eddy Fulbright. He's a well-known drug dealer and been arrested for rape. The witnesses seem to disappear before they can testify."

Riley leaned back in his chair. A rapist, now a killer. Riley's heart sped up its tempo. "Any location on him?"

"No." Voices sounded in the phone's background, along with more shuffling of footsteps. "There's more."

"I'm sure. Otherwise, why the big secret?"

"He's a narc for the feds. Some of us are still looking for him, but it's on the side. The DEA wants the investigation killed for right now." More voices came from the background. "I'll call you after I get off work and fill you in on more."

Fulbright, being an informant for the feds, explained why no one was in a big hurry to arrest the guy. Probably involved in something big. Once he gave the government what they wanted, they'd turn him over to the local authorities. Unless he made a deal for full immunity. Riley hated that thought. As long as Fulbright was loose, Calley was in danger. He snatched his phone back up.

"Matthew, this is Riley. You still got friends in the DEA?"

"Sure. What do you need?"

"The location of one of their narcs. Apparently, he's the guy who killed Ms. Martinez, and might be after Calley Regan."

Riley straightened. "What makes you think that?"

"Word on the street is he was bragging about twenty thousand he received to get rid of someone."

A SLIGHT BREEZE KEPT the wonderful August morning from being hot. Calley's hair blew in front of her face. The sun was bright blue overhead. The green trees gave off a hint of pine fragrance. She inhaled a breath of fresh air.

"This was a good idea, if I say so myself." BJ finished her last bite of bagel. "Did you get enough to eat?"

"Yes." Calley wiped her hands on a napkin. "Thank you."

"Have you come up with any names for the baby now that you know it's a boy?"

"I've looked on the Internet at a few sites, but nothing's hit me yet." Calley used her finger to scrap up cream cheese from her plate. If it had been a girl, she'd have named her Eva, but with it being a boy, she didn't know what to call him.

"I'm sure you'll know it when you see it."

"I hope so." The day was so nice, and Calley was restless. "Would you like to go for a walk?"

"I think that's a fine idea. I'll just clean this up and put on my walking shoes."

BJ rose, took up the dishes and headed inside the house while Calley continued to sit at the picnic table. Everything smelled so fresh. A broad-winged hawk hollered overhead. Its dark wings contrasted with the blue sky. It glided through the air with no effort. What it must be like to be that free.

"Calley." A man's whisper startled her. She spun.

"Peter." She gasped.

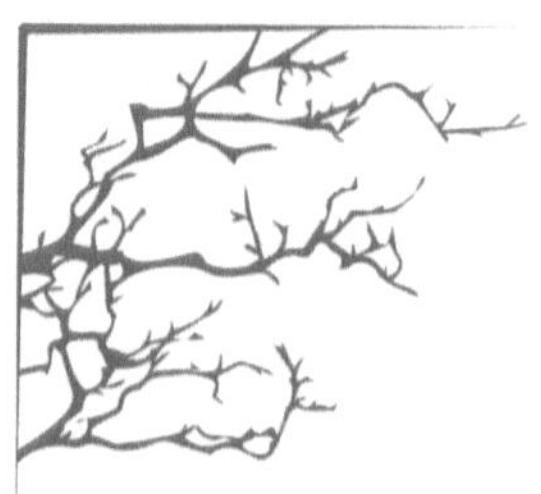

10

Riley couldn't get the vision out of his mind. The sound of gunfire echoed in his memory. Police swarmed into the bank. Paramedics rushed about. Someone had tried to stop him from entering, but he shoved around them. The metallic smell of blood mixed with gunpowder almost overtook him. His pulse stopped. The woman he loved more than life lay on the floor. No movement. He rushed over to her. Beth was already gone. There were no last words. No chance for him to say he was sorry for not being there for her. He didn't know how long he held her before they pulled her away. It was the last time he recalled crying.

Riley stared at the cross in the sanctuary's front. He had failed before with Beth. How was he going to protect Calley? Especially since he couldn't locate the whereabouts of the guy who had killed Eva? *God, help me figure this out. She and the baby need you more than they need me right now.* The door to the room closed behind him. When he turned, Matthew stood in the back. The tattoo on the minister's neck sneaked out over his collar.

"I saw you come in." He came forward and sat next to Riley. "I didn't want to disturb you, but you looked like you lost your dog or something. And I know you don't own one."

"You getting nervous?" Riley didn't want to admit the reason for his visit was Calley. "The wedding is less than a week away."

"I want it over with. I can't wait to be Lydia's husband." He grinned. "How's Calley doing?"

"So far so good."

"You find Eddy Fulbright?"

Riley shook his head. "Everyone's keeping pretty tight-lipped. I just hope he doesn't come after Calley, but she's the only witness. And I imagine he's not happy she shot him." He raised his eyes to the cross. *Please protect her.*

"Calley's a strong woman," Matthew said. "There's sheer determination to keep her child safe. Otherwise, she wouldn't have had a gun when that guy broke into her place."

"Yeah."

"I get the feeling you like her."

"What's not to like? She's got a good sense of humor, she's friendly to just about everyone, and like you said, she's strong."

"But?"

"But what?" Riley leaned forward, his arms on his legs.

"I sense some hesitation." Matthew patted Riley on the shoulder. "Lydia told me a bit about your girlfriend who died. You wanna talk about it?"

Riley raised himself up. "She was more than a girlfriend. We were a month away from getting married when she got killed." His throat tightened.

"A robbery at a bank, I understand."

Riley nodded. He shouldn't have stopped in. The last thing he wanted to do was discuss Beth.

"Must have been hard not being able to save her." Matthew leaned back and crossed his ankle over his knee.

"By the time I got there, it was too late." Riley swallowed hard. "I was supposed to take her to lunch. If I hadn't let the job get in the way, she wouldn't have been there."

"It's not your fault."

"I know that in my head. It's the rest of me I have yet to convince."

"And now Calley, a woman you have interest in, is having problems."

Riley's face warmed. Was he that transparent? "What makes you think I have that type of interest in Calley?"

"The way you look at her and the fact she's at your house right now. I'm not a genius by any means, but I figured it out." Matthew laughed. "To be honest, Lydia figured it out. And I think Sheryl told her."

"Great." Just what he wanted, a bunch of gossip.

"Don't worry. It's not going to hurt you to be interested in a woman," Matthew said. "And for everyone to know about it. Might keep Marylou from continually buying up all the okra in town. From what I hear, it's her best dish, and she thinks it's your favorite."

"I want Calley and the baby to be safe." Riley rose. He glanced one last time at the cross before he walked out with Matthew following. "It's got nothing to do with interest."

"It's okay to move on with your life. You have to stop shutting yourself off from the rest of the world because of something tragic in your past."

"It seems everyone near me dies." Riley slapped his hat from one hand to another. "Beth, Lydia's husband Justin, my parents. I'd hate to see anything bad happen to Calley or her baby."

"Have faith. If it's God's will, everything will work out. Ask yourself a question. Do you wish you'd never met Beth? Was the pain worth being with her for even one day?"

Riley raised his eyebrows. He walked from the church without answering. What if it wasn't God's will that Calley survive? How could he protect her if God wanted to take her?

And how could he live with himself if he didn't stop that from happening?

"PETER, WHAT ARE YOU doing here?" Calley's heart pounded in her chest. She glanced around to see if anyone saw him. He stood a few feet from the bench she sat on. He was still as good looking as when she'd seen him last. His blue eyes shined, and he'd combed his blond hair back from his face. He reminded her of a male model. His blue polo shirt and khaki Dockers fit to a tee.

What did she think would happen in the months since she'd last seen him? That he'd get fat and grow warts all over his face?

"I'm a lawyer. There isn't anyone I can't find." He smiled with perfect white teeth. How had she not noticed his arrogance before now?

"What do you want?" She straightened her shoulders and raised her chin.

"I heard about Eva. I just wanted to check on you."

"You could have called."

"I had to see for myself that you were all right." He walked forward and took hold of her hand, but she jerked away. "I know I hurt you, Calley, but it doesn't mean I don't care."

"I stopped caring the day you told me you were married."

He took a step back. "I should have told you earlier. Everything just happened so fast with us."

"From the way your wife sounded when she threatened me, I wasn't the first. Probably won't be the last."

He stared up at the sky. He didn't seem fazed at all over what his wife had done. "You're different, Calley. But when you told me about the baby, I got scared."

"And now?"

"I've been thinking about it. You said you were going to take care of it. Since there's no more kid, we can go back to the way we were."

The picnic table hid her belly from view. He didn't know. Anger grew inside her at his thoughts. "No more — If I had known you had a wife, there would never have been an *us*. You don't honestly think I'd go back to where we were, do you? When I said I'd take care of the baby, I meant raise it without your help."

His expression turned into a scowl. "I thought you had an abortion."

She scooted up from the bench. "Apparently not." She stood. Her belly protruded from under her shirt.

He took hold of her arm. His eyes turned dark and cold. It happened so fast, Calley wondered how often she'd missed this side of Peter. "If you think I'm going to pay support for some brat you tried to trap me with, you can think again." His grip tightened. "I'll not lose my family over this."

"Ow. You're hurting me."

"I suggest you let go of her before I put a hole in you the size of a silver dollar." BJ stood on the back patio, a rifle in her hands aimed in Peter's direction. "And if you have any doubts, you might want to check out the trophy collection in my room first."

Peter released his hold on Calley.

"Is he the man who killed Eva?" BJ asked.

"No, I'm not." Peter's arrogance shined through.

Calley shook her head.

"It was just a slight misunderstanding," Peter said. "I got carried away. I didn't mean any harm. My name's Peter Jameson." Peter held out his hand in greeting.

"Well, you just get carried away off my property before I shoot you for trespassing."

Peter glared at BJ, then Calley. "I meant what I said about that kid. Don't play with me. I can be a very dangerous man if you make me angry."

"I don't want anything from you," Calley said. She refused to cry. He was no longer worth it. What kind of mess had she made of her life? "You stay away from me, and we'll get along fine."

He shot another glance at BJ, then turned on his heel and stormed back into the woods.

Calley's hands trembled, and her knees weakened.

"It's okay, child." BJ placed her arm around Calley's shoulder. "Everything's going to be all right."

"He's the baby's father. I can't believe I thought I was in love with him."

"We all make mistakes when it comes to men." BJ led her inside to a chair at the dining room table. "Here, wipe your eyes. I'll call Riley and let him know what happened."

"No." Calley jumped up. "Please, don't."

"But he threatened you. Could he have paid for someone to come after you, and they got Eva by mistake?"

Calley hated that thought. "He had no reason to. He thought I had an abortion." Calley stomped her foot, then fell back down into the seat. "How could I have screwed up my life so bad? Not just mine, but my baby's, too. Maybe my mom is right."

"No. She's not. You're a wonderful person, Calley Regan, and don't you ever forget it." BJ pulled up a chair beside Calley and took hold of her hand. "Now, what's the real reason you don't want Riley to know?"

"It's not just him. Everyone will know in time I'm an unwed mother. I don't want them to know the father." Calley paused. Would BJ think less of her? "He's married," she whispered.

"Did you know when you first started seeing him?"

"No. I didn't find out until I was pregnant." Calley let out a heavy breath. "It's just one more screw up. How am I ever going to raise a child when I don't even have control over my own life?"

RILEY PULLED INTO THE driveway. It'd been a long day, and he wanted nothing more than to eat and get working on his bike to relieve some of the tension. Matthew's question swirled around his mind throughout the rest of the day. Memories of Beth weighed on his mind all day. He had loved her, and no matter the outcome, he wouldn't have given up one moment with her.

He sat in the car and stared at the house. Shadowy figures moved about inside. Calley's silhouette was evident. Why did he feel a jump in his gut whenever he saw her? She and Beth were so different. Beth was goal-oriented and knew what she wanted from life. Calley, at times, acted like a child and didn't seem to have much order in her life. They did have one thing in common. They were both strong. Beth with her sense of right and wrong, and Calley with her loyalty, especially to an unborn child. It would have been easy for her to take the fast way out, but she chose not to. He smiled. And somehow, she made him want to live again.

He stopped halfway up the steps. A vehicle approached down the long gravel driveway. Marylou honked and waved her fingers at him. Great, just what he needed. In the passenger seat was her friend Tiffany. Riley didn't know her well. At least she didn't bathe in perfume like Marylou.

"Riley!" Marylou yelled with her window down. She shot out of her car and walked up to him, a package in her hands. "When I made some okra last night, I decided to bring some by."

"Thanks." He forced himself to keep from rolling his eyes. "Hello, Tiffany." He was hoping later to go for a test drive on the motorcycle once he worked out a few kinks. He opened the door and allowed the two women inside. It was going to be a long night.

"What brings you two ladies by?" BJ pulled her head up from the oven. Calley was setting plates on the table. "Calley, I believe you met both Marylou and Tiffany at the shower."

"Yes, I did. How are you?" Calley said.

"We're awesome. We've been to the gym. Need to keep our figures."

Riley caught the hint of sarcasm in Marylou's voice. The narrowing of Calley's eyes said she noticed it also. Riley strolled back to his room. He removed his tie from around his neck and unbuttoned the top button of his shirt. Murmur of talk from the kitchen area drifted in, but he couldn't make out what they were saying over the clatter of dishes being moved about.

"Hey." Calley stuck her head in his opened door. "Would you like a soda or sweet tea for dinner?"

"Tea will be fine." He leaned toward her. "And by the way, your figure's just fine."

Her face beamed. Giving her reason to glow like that eased some of the day's tension. He leaned an arm over his head on the doorjamb and watched her walk away. She really was a pretty lady.

"Will you be joining us for dinner?"

Riley wanted to strangle her. How was he to enjoy his meal when Marylou's harsh fragrance would be hanging all over him?

"Oh, that's so sweet of you." Marylou's voice dripped sugar. "We'd love to join you. Right Tiff?"

"Why don't you place your dish on a trivet in the center of the table?"

Riley walked from his room. The four women bumped and trip around each other as they finished setting food on the table. For the first time since he'd arrived, he noticed dark circles curved under Calley's eyes. He'd awakened to hear her walking to the kitchen in the middle of the night. He couldn't be sure whether she was having a hard time because of the baby or Eva's death. It would take time until she worked through seeing her friend die.

"How was your day, Riley?" She said when he took a place at the head of the table.

"Busy."

"He's such a gem to talk to, isn't he?" She leaned over to Marylou, who had walked around the table and dropped into the chair next to Riley.

"Oh, he's just quiet. Never been one to gossip." She looked Calley up and down. "Boy, when I heard you were pregnant, I hadn't realized just how so. When's the baby due?"

"About two months now."

"Wow. Have you got a dress for the wedding?" Tiffany had a smug look on her face. "I bet it's hard to find one that fits right and is flattering."

"I have one, but thanks for asking." Calley's cheeks reddened. Riley couldn't tell if it was embarrassment or anger.

"What are your plans once the baby is born?" Marylou sipped from her drink, leaving a lipstick print where her lips had touched the glass. "I'm sure you don't expect to stay here. There's really not enough room for three adults and a baby. Besides, with Riley's schedule, I can't imagine a baby crying in the middle of the night would be a good thing."

Riley hadn't considered Calley leaving once she had the baby. In a short period, he'd gotten used to seeing her in the morning before he left for work and having her here in the evenings. The idea of her going away left a hole in the pit of his stomach. He didn't have much of an appetite anymore.

"Don't you worry about Calley and this baby." BJ patted Calley on her arm. "She's welcome to stay as long as she likes. I'm kind of looking forward to having a little one around. Riley's gotten too big to order around."

"Yeah, but you still try." Riley spoke without looking up.

"Got to try to keep you in line. Even at your age."

BJ and Calley both laughed.

Marylou placed her hand on Riley's arm. "But Calley doesn't strike me as the type who would want to be a burden."

"She isn't," Riley said. "And she's not a burden."

A appeared on Calley's face as she looked down at her plate.

Marylou stroked Riley's arm. "Another reason I stopped by was to see how you were coming with your toast for the wedding?"

If he hadn't lost his appetite before, he sure did then. With everything going on with Calley, he'd forgotten about his toast. "I haven't had time to think about it much."

"You haven't? Riley, the wedding is this Saturday. Well, it's a good thing I came by. I've written up some ideas I thought I'd let you look at." Marylou pulled out a piece of paper from her jeans pocket. "This one talks about how you're such good friends, and this one is about Matthew and Lydia are made for each other. The one in the back goes into love and all that stuff."

"They're awful long, aren't they?" Riley glanced at the pages. Each toast filled a page. Did she honestly think he'd want to stand up and talk this long? He certainly didn't need anyone telling him what to say to two of his closest friends. His appetite had vanished.

"I think you should keep it short and simple," Calley said. "Something from your heart about how you feel about the couple."

"Short?" Tiffany rolled her eyes. "It's obvious you haven't been to many weddings. Next to the ceremony, the toasts are the most important parts."

A mouthful of pork stuck in Riley's throat. He wasn't sure if the toast was as important as Tiffany indicated, but it sure didn't help his nerves any.

"Does anyone need any more tea?" Calley rose and walked to the kitchen.

"Oh my. Are you having trouble walking?" Tiffany asked.

"No, why?" Calley returned to the table carrying the pitcher.

"It's just that... I'm sorry. I don't want to sound mean, but you're waddling."

Tiffany and Marylou leaned over to each other and giggled. BJ's lips tightened. Riley shot her a glare so she wouldn't say anything. Calley could take care of herself.

"It's the baby," Calley said. "He's kind of hard to carry, so it makes me walk funny."

"I imagine. Kind of like being fat, huh?" A smug look came across Tiffany's face.

Anger rose in Riley. Before he could open his mouth, tea splashed across the table and into Tiffany's face.

She let out a yell. "This is a cashmere sweater. It's ruined. I'll never get the tea stains out."

"Oh, I am sorry." Calley said. "Since becoming pregnant, I've been so clumsy." She walked around the table with a handful of napkins and patted Tiffany down. "I'll be more than happy to pay you for your sweater."

"You bet you will."

"Just get me the receipt. I don't want to pay full price if you bought it used." Calley's jaw tightened. "How about you, Marylou? Anything of yours I can replace?"

Marylou was speechless. She had her mouth opened, but no sound came out. It was the first time Riley had ever seen her like this. He tried not to laugh as he piled potatoes on his plate. His appetite had somehow returned.

CALLEY FOUGHT THE URGE to strangle Tiffany. How dare that woman say she waddled? Just because it was true didn't mean she had to say it out loud. Besides, she had no control over what her pregnant body did. If Tiffany wanted to insult someone, why not go after her good friend Marylou, who hung over Riley all during dinner? She couldn't have been more obvious. The house still reeked of her cheap perfume. And when she wiped her mouth, half her lips remained on the napkin.

She heard the murmur of Marylou, Tiffany, and Riley talking in the garage. It was just like in high school. The pretty girls teasing her just to make themselves feel better. Tears formed in Calley's eyes as she put the glasses in the dishwasher.

BJ had allowed Tiffany to borrow clothes while she tried to wash the tea stains out. Calley stood upright and looked down. She *was* huge. Her feet used to be visible from her, but not anymore. She let out a sigh and swallowed back her tears. Once she had the baby, she would get back into her exercise routine. She'd show that mean Tiffany.

"Tiffany. Tiffany," Calley said with a smirk. "Who cares what someone named after a jewelry store has to say?"

"That was really something. I hadn't noticed you being so clumsy before." BJ laughed as she entered the room. "And that remark about the shirt being used was priceless."

"It's an older style that came out years ago. I can't imagine she just bought it." Calley turned away so BJ couldn't see her getting emotional.

"What's wrong, child?"

"I don't know. I hate people like Tiffany. Always making fun of others. I know I'm fat, she doesn't have to point it out."

"You're not fat. You're having a baby." She pulled Calley's chin toward her. "And Tiffany is a spoiled brat who needed to be taken down a peg. You did just that."

A roar in the garage caught their attention.

"I guess Riley's got the bike going," BJ said.

Cheers came through the closed door.

"Come on." BJ patted Calley's arm. "Let's see if it's drivable. He's been working on it for a long time."

Calley followed BJ out. Riley sat on the seat of the bike, a black helmet over his head. He took off out the raised garage door down the gravel road. BJ rushed to the driveway and watched him while Marylou, Tiffany, and Calley waited for his return inside the garage.

Marylou's phone rang, and she glanced at the screen. She walked into the corner to answer the call. Calley walked to the raised garage door, hoping to avoid any type of confrontation with Tiffany.

"I don't care what it takes. I've given you some of half the money already. Just get the job done! I want to get on with my life." Marylou barked. After her call, she returned to Tiffany's side. "Trouble with a contractor."

Calley was glad to see Marylou had trouble with someone other than her.

"I wonder if Riley will give me a ride," Marylou said. She turned to Calley. "I guess you're not in any shape. Are you?"

"It'd be like having a watermelon stuck between the two of them." Tiffany smirked at Calley.

"Yeah." Marylou giggled. "But I can get real close, with my arms around him." She got close to Calley's face.

Calley rolled her eyes. If she hadn't been pregnant, she'd have considered giving one of them a black eye. She learned a long time ago pretty girls cared what they looked like. A punch in the face usually worked wonders for adjusting their attitudes.

Instead, she withdrew inside to her bedroom and reclined on the bed. The motorcycle engine died down in the garage, and the door lowered. Riley must have had some trouble with it or he wouldn't have returned so soon. As bad as that was for Riley, the fact that Marylou couldn't ride behind him gave Calley a sense of relief. Her eyes drifted closed.

The baby shifted, waking Calley from a sound sleep. She heard a noise in the kitchen and hoped Marylou and Tiffany were no longer there. She glanced at the clock. It was nearing eleven.

"Great, now you decide to bounce on the bladder." She rose and crawled from bed.

When she walked from her room, a cascade of light from the dining room shadowed the hallway. The noise of someone crumpling paper caught her attention. Once she finished with the bathroom, she stuck her head around the corner. Riley sat at the dining room table. His elbows were bent, and his hands rested in his hair. He let out a heavy breath.

"You sound like a man with a lot on his mind." Calley walked up behind him. The aroma of his soap glided into her sinuses. The musky smell enveloped her. She hoped she wasn't obvious when she breathed it in.

"I'm trying to get my toast written. I've run out of time." He crumpled up another piece of paper. "Getting up in front of all those people is not something I'm looking forward to."

"You? Mr. Attention-Seeker?" Calley walked into the kitchen and grabbed a bottle of water from the refrigerator.

He laughed and leaned back in his chair.

"She's wrong," Calley said.

"Who?"

"Your girlfriend, Marylou. I've been to a lot of weddings, and the only time the toast has been long is when the best man is drunk."

"She's not my girlfriend." His lips tightened.

"Okay. Your wanna-be girlfriend. She makes that pretty obvious." Calley took a seat next to Riley. "Let me see what you have." She opened a crumpled piece of paper from the garbage pile and shook her head.

"That bad?" He tossed the pen down.

"No. You're just trying too hard. Besides, this isn't you."

"What do you mean?"

"You're trying to be fancy, poetic. Just be yourself. If you could be alone in a room with Lydia and Matthew, what two sentences would you say to them to convey how you feel?" She rose. "That's all you have to do."

"Two sentences?"

"Yeah. Two sentences." She leaned into Riley's ear. "I think your wanna-be girlfriend was showing off." Calley laughed and walked off a few steps, then stopped and turned. "What's wrong with the motorcycle?"

"What do you mean?"

"You were only out for a brief ride. Did something happen to it?"

"No. It runs great."

"Marylou said she was going to try to convince you to take her for a ride." Calley felt her grip tighten on the arm of the chair as she thought of that woman holding onto Riley. "She mentioned it in the garage."

"She asked, but I told her it wasn't safe yet."

"Oh." Calley's feet slid on the wood floor.

"Besides," Riley's voice caused her to stop. "She isn't the one I want riding behind me."

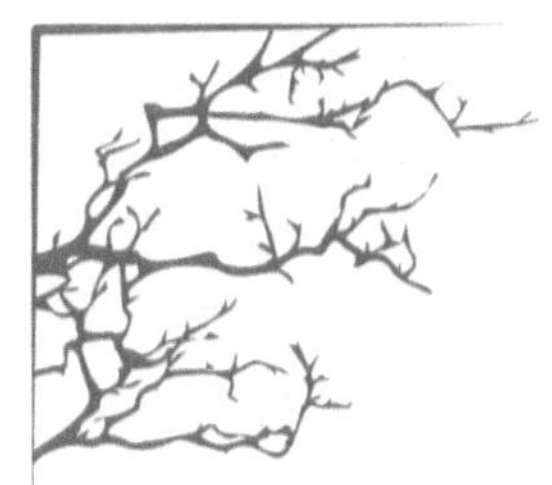

11

Calley sat in her car and stared out at the people walking into the church. They all looked so nice in their dresses. She looked like a blimp. Temptation rose to put the car in reverse and head out.

BJ had gotten a frantic call to pick something up for the wedding, and Riley had to be at the church early to play best man. With her luck, Marylou and Tiffany would be in there, waiting to tease her. If she hadn't promised Riley and Lydia she'd be there, she'd leave.

Might as well get it over with.

She opened the car door, rose from the car, and adjusted the dress. Maybe she didn't look as huge as she felt. She was headed for the door when she stopped in her tracks. Uncle Joe. Her throat went dry as if drinking a glass of sand. He nodded in her direction, and she froze in place. Why was he still considered a member of the family, yet she wasn't? He wasn't even blood related, just a close friend of her father's. Beside him stood Allison, her mother, and another man Calley didn't know. The stranger looked her way when Calley's mother pointed in her direction.

"That's James Newman, III."

Calley jolted and spun. Her Aunt Celeste stood behind her. She wore a light pink dress, and her hair was up in a bun on the back of her head. Even at her age, she looked wonderful.

"He's one of the deacons here at the church. He's also a city councilman. Tell me. Doesn't he look just like a politician? He reeks of arrogance."

Her aunt was right. He looked like an elected official with his painted-on smile and pseudo-friendly look. He even had shifty eyes.

95

"I'm so glad you could make it." Celeste placed her arm around Calley and led her into the church. "Lydia told us about the attack. How are you holding up?"

"I'm doing better." Calley kept her voice low. "Thank you." She wasn't sure if she was thanking her aunt for asking about the attack or leading her past her mother and uncle.

"By the way, we didn't invite him." She gave Calley a squeeze. "But the card said your mother could bring a guest. It doesn't take much for people to see why my sister and I don't get along very well."

Calley nodded. "I thought you'd be in with Lydia in the back room. You *are* the mother of the bride."

"I forgot something in the car. I thought I'd rush out before I got seated." Celeste dragged Calley with her to the front row and moved her into a pew. "I'm glad Lydia decided to go with something smaller. It would feel overdone if she'd gone for a big affair. We loved Justin very much, and when he died, we didn't think she'd ever be happy again. But Matthew, he's a good man."

Over her shoulder, Calley caught sight of Uncle Joe as he walked in the door to the sanctuary. It surprised her he didn't burst into flames. Her mother's smug look faced Calley as she pointed for Allison to sit in the pew behind Calley and Celeste. Allison gave Calley's shoulder a squeeze as she passed. Uncle Joe again nodded in her direction. Calley gave a quick glance to the exit on her left.

"Celeste," Mom's snide tone grated Calley's nerves.

"Nanette." Celeste replied, then leaned toward Calley. "Now, don't you worry about them. You just stay here with me, and they won't bother you. I imagine my husband is not going to be thrilled when he sees Joe here, either."

"Maybe I should go," Calley said. "I don't want anything to ruin Lydia's day."

"You not being here would ruin it." She continued to whisper. "Besides, if anyone ruins it, it'll be that sister of mine." She grinned.

"Enough of them. Tell me what's been going on with you? Besides the baby and the incident in Atlanta, what else is new?"

"Nothing much. Riley Owens has taken it upon himself to be my guard and protector."

"To be honest, there are a lot worse looking protectors out there."

Calley laughed. "Yeah, there are. Love him in that cowboy hat." Both women giggled.

She stared at the beautiful white gardenias in the front. Their fragrance cascaded over the entire area. They had always been Lydia's favorite. Calley recalled as a teen, sneaking into a neighbor's yard and picking the largest gardenia for Lydia's birthday gift. The old woman was mad until she found out Calley had given her prized flower away as a gift. She told Calley she was very thoughtful, but next time to not pick any without asking.

Blue streamers hung down from gardenia bulbs surrounded by pearls at each pew. Sheryl had done a wonderful job decorating.

Riley walked through a door on the opposite side of the church, followed by Matthew and another man. They stood up front dressed in black suits. Riley kept running his hand through his hair and shifting from foot to foot. Whether in a tan sheriff's uniform or a suit, her aunt was right. He did look good. Of course, her favorite outfit for him was jeans and a t-shirt. That's when he looked most relaxed. Calley gave him a wave of her fingers when he glanced in her direction. He nodded and winked in return. She instantly felt better.

"I think Riley's about to have a heart attack." Calley leaned over to her aunt.

Celeste laughed. "He almost looks like he's melting with the amount of sweat he's losing."

Calley glanced over her shoulder. Her mother was in a corner speaking with James Newman, the man she'd been with outside. They both looked Calley's way. A shiver ran up her back. She forced her attention to band up front.

Matthew held a grin on his face. Not a small one either. He continually looked to the back doors of the church. Probably waiting for his bride. Calley assumed he was ready to get this over with. She could tell from the anxious look on Riley's face he certainly was.

The music began, and everyone stood. The first bridesmaid, Matthew's sister, walked out, followed by Sheryl. Both women wore royal blue full-length off-the-shoulder dresses. Behind them came Lydia on her father's arm. She walked out in a Pnina Tornai wedding gown. It was an ivory v-neck which crisscrossed her body, accentuating her small waist. Lydia had gone to New York to purchase it. There'd be no way Calley would ever fit into a dress like that. Pregnant or not. Not that she'd want to spend that kind of money. She'd just as soon elope and use the money for a nice honeymoon.

The wedding was wonderful. Calley kept waiting for Riley to faint, but he never did. As everyone stood to allow the newly married couple to walk down the aisle, Calley caught her mother's sneer from the pew behind her. Another chill raced through Calley, yet she didn't know why.

RILEY WAS TIRED OF posing for pictures. Matthew and Lydia, Lydia and her parents, Matthew and his family. The wedding party. He and Matthew. It was all ridiculous. This suit, combined with the heat, wasn't helping his mood. He needed a cold drink. But that would mean going inside. The sooner they got inside, the closer it came for him to get up in front of everyone. Why couldn't he get an emergency call? Where's a robbery when he needed one?

"You look pale there." Sheryl chuckled as she patted his shoulder. "You really aren't enjoying yourself. Are you?"

"Not really my cup of tea."

"I could tell. I thought you were going to fall over as I walked down the aisle." She shook her head. "The idea of having to hold you up during the ceremony didn't sound very pleasing."

"I made it." He'd hoped his anxiety wasn't that apparent. Good thing he wasn't an actor.

"I'm very proud of you for that." She grinned. "Keeping your eyes on Calley must have helped."

He let out a slow release of air to calm his anger. Sheryl was one of the biggest gossips in town. If she was digging for information, she'd come to the wrong person. "What's Calley got to do with anything?"

"Nothing. I'm just saying I noticed you looking at her most of the time." Sheryl nudged him with her elbow. "Chill out. I think it's great. Calley's a wonderful person."

He agreed but didn't say so. The last thing he wanted was for it to be all over town.

"She's had it rough, running away when she was sixteen. It couldn't have been easy to finish high school and go to college without any family support."

Riley listened with great interest. He knew little about Calley's life, especially her younger years. Finishing school showed how strong and determined she really was.

"I'm glad you like her. You both deserve to be happy." Sheryl leaned into his ear and whispered, "By the way, she couldn't seem to keep her eyes off you either."

As Sheryl walk away, he hoped she was right. The thought of Calley ever leaving made his heart feel empty.

CELESTE HAD TO GO WITH the wedding party to get her picture taken, leaving Calley to fend for herself. She headed toward the back of the church where the reception would take place. The quicker she got in and got to a table, the less chance there was of bumping into people she didn't want to see.

"I was surprised to see you here."

Calley's blood ran cold when she turned to face Uncle Joe. "I'm surprised you had the guts to show up."

"Now, now. What's in the past is in the past," he said. He glanced down at her belly. "We've both made mistakes."

Calley folded her arms over her stomach. "Just leave me alone." She kept her voice down so people passing couldn't hear. The last thing she wanted to do was make a scene.

"As you wish. I thought we could sit somewhere and clear the air." He touched her arm, and Calley jerked away. "I know I hurt you, but I've found Jesus. I'd like to make amends."

"Just because you're standing in a church doesn't make you a godly man." Her voice quivered. She bit her tongue to keep from crying. "Excuse me."

She shifted around him and headed inside the reception room. BJ waved to her from a table in the back. Calley's hands trembled as she picked up a glass for a sip of water once she sat down. She didn't care whether Uncle Joe had found Jesus. From what she heard, once a molester, always a molester. She'd just relaxed when James Newman headed her way. The large grin on his face made her feel like a canary about to be devoured by a cat.

"BJ, how are you this fine afternoon?" He leaned over and took her hand.

"I'm doing wonderful. James, this is Calley, Lydia's cousin."

"Nice to meet you." His hands were chilly and wet when he shook Calley's. "I believe I met your mother earlier." He slithered down into a chair next to her. "She told me about your predicament. It must be a hard thing to go through on your own."

Her *predicament.* Calley fought to keep from laughing out loud. She glimpsed Riley when he walked in the door. He sat at a long table near the front with Sheryl and other members of the bridal party. If only they could sit together.

"I don't know if you're aware of it, but my wife and I lost our only child last year. Our son. It involved that whole mess Lydia had to contend with." Tears stood at attention in his eyes, showing he still hadn't gotten over the loss.

"I'm sorry about your son," Calley said. Her heart ached for him. She knew that pain from losing Eva. It was like losing a sister.

"Thank you." He inhaled deeply. "I understand you're having a boy."

"Yes."

"I'd like to discuss an opportunity with you at a later date. The prospect of maybe raising that child for you. After all, a boy needs a man around the house." Words slid from his lips like oil on a Teflon pan.

Calley shifted back in her chair. An uneasy feeling crept in. This man was looking for a replacement for his dead son.

BJ shot out of her chair. "I can't believe you would come up and say something like that. Especially here, at a wedding."

"I'm just letting her know there are alternatives. Most women can't raise a boy to be a man. That's proven by all the crime in this country."

He turned his sleazy smile back to Calley. She knew what a mouse felt like in a rattler's cage. Riley walked her way, which eased her tension.

"It's something you need to think about." He rose from his seat, apparently unaware of Riley's presence. "It's a fact that most of the men in jail were raised by single mothers. Boys need a man to show them how to be a man. It takes a lot of time and an extremely strong woman to do that."

Riley's hands turned to fists. "If we go by your generalization, then every boy raised by a man would be a good one. So, what happened to yours?"

James spun around. "You know very well what happened wasn't our fault. He was getting himself together when he died."

"He had enough crack in his system to last a weekend." Riley took a step toward Calley and placed a hand on her shoulder. "If Calley gave this child up for adoption, the last person she'd give it to is you."

James opened his mouth to speak but said nothing. Instead, he stalked off to the table where Calley's mom sat. He leaned over and spoke to her. Nanette's glare nearly scalded Calley's skin. It was obvious who instigated the whole adoption thing. How could her mother be so cruel?

"Come on, you two," Riley said.

"Where are we going?" Calley pushed herself up from the chair.

"You and BJ are moving to the front table." He placed his hand on her back. "If I have to give this toast, I need all the support I can get."

RILEY COULDN'T EAT the chicken in front of him. His stomach was already in a knot. Anything inside would only make him more nauseated. His foot tapped a steady beat on the wood floor. Calley sat to his left, between him and Ty Davenport, a former co-worker of Matthew's. Ty had worked undercover on several drug stings so he could have information on Eddy Fulbright. Riley hoped to get Ty cornered later to see if he could get a lead on the guy.

"I can't believe how nervous you are." Sheryl sat in the chair on the other side of him. "If you'd like, I'll say something extra. As the maid of honor, it won't look too weird. Besides, I'd hate for you to pass out."

"Oh, come on," Calley said. "Marylou would love the opportunity to give him mouth-to-mouth."

He couldn't help but laugh. "That's all right. I can do this."

"Remember what I said." Calley leaned over to him. "Just say what's in your heart."

For a reason he didn't understand, some of the tension eased. He wasn't sure if it was because of her words or just because she was next to him. He reached over and gave her hand a squeeze.

"We need a group photo for the wedding album." Rayleene Davenport, the photographer, and Ty's wife, held a camera with a long lens up to her face.

"Wait a moment," Sheryl said. "We're missing someone."

"Who?" Rayleene glanced around the guests.

"You, silly." Sheryl motioned to Rayleene's helper. "Get him over here so you can stand next to your husband."

Riley leaned his arm on the back of Calley's chair, and she moved closer to him. The others stood around them.

"Let me see those teeth." The young man said, holding up the camera. "That means you, best man."

"Or I'll call Marylou over here," Calley whispered in Riley's ear.

Riley again laughed. How was this woman able to get him to relax and enjoy himself? He continued to lean toward her, even after everyone else sat back down. He enjoyed her closeness. The subtle scent of her perfume calmed him even more.

Twenty minutes later, the dinner was over, and the wedding planner nodded in Riley's direction. He blew out a deep breath of air and returned the nod.

"Here goes nothing." He gave Calley's hand another squeeze, stood, and tapped his spoon against the wineglass to get everyone's attention. "I'd just like to say a few words about the bride and groom." He looked over at Matthew and Lydia, who sat at the front table with their parents. "I know you two have been through a lot these last few years, but I'm happy to say you've finally discovered happiness again. I wish you both the best in the future. No two people deserve it more." He raised his glass and tossed down the drink, then sat. Everyone else followed.

"Thank you." Lydia mouthed, and Matthew nodded in his direction.

He glanced over at Sheryl, then to Calley. "Too short?"

"I thought it was perfect," Calley said.

"For you, it was just right. I'll be a bit longer." Sheryl gave him a large grin.

Riley felt his shoulders release. He was glad that was over.

After Sheryl gave her toast, they did the dances. Father/daughter, mother-in-law/son-in-law. Since Matthew had no mother, he danced with his sister. Then everyone was offered the chance to dance.

"Riley."

He looked up as Marylou neared. Her lipstick smeared around her mouth. "What a wonderful short toast. I was surprised to see you didn't use something I prepared."

"I got better advice."

"Well, the least you can do is dance with me since I went through all that work."

"It'll have to be later." Riley stood and held his hand out to Calley. "This one's for Calley."

"Are you sure she should dance in her condition?" Marylou placed her hand against her throat. "I'd hate for her to go into labor."

"Don't worry about me. This kid isn't ready yet." Calley jumped up from her chair and grinned. She took Riley's hand, and he led her to the dance floor.

Her purple dress wrapped around her waist, and a silver pin connected to the side. She'd pulled her hair up from her face into a fancy hairstyle with soft curls surrounding her face. Riley recalled having to catch his breath when he'd first seen her that morning.

"By the way, you look wonderful." His heart pounded in his chest when he wrapped his arm around her. "That's a good color for you."

"Thank you."

"No, thank you for saving me." He leaned his cheek against the side of her head. "I'll eventually have to give in and dance with Marylou, but for now, I'm safe."

"That's the least of your worries. You're out here on the dance floor with a very pregnant woman. I'm assuming the gossips will be in full force tonight."

"Let 'em talk." He whirled her around. "In fact, it'll actually give them something to talk about." The baby between them made dancing awkward. Riley's heart skipped a beat when he pulled her near.

CALLEY CLUNG TO RILEY'S arm. It felt so good to be held by a man, especially one as nice as Riley. She knew it wouldn't be forever, but she could enjoy it, if only for right now. Why couldn't she have met him before Peter? Things might have turned out different. Riley had yet to return them to the table. He'd danced almost every song with her so far, even the fast ones. Not that she could get too wild, but it was nice to have some fun. This was the final song before Matthew and Lydia planned to leave. She was glad for a slow one.

She leaned her head against Riley's chin. He whispered the words to the song playing. Chris Young's "The Man I Want to Be." Tears raised in Calley's eyes. Would she ever find a man who wanted to be better for her? No, she was the one who needed to improve. The baby gave her a swift kick as if to say, "Stop being such a romantic fool".

He pulled back when the song finished. "Are you all right?"

"Yeah. I just need to use the restroom."

She rushed to the back of the reception hall. The bathroom was decorated with the same ribbon ornaments as the sanctuary had been. Sheryl had gone all out. Tempted to stick her head in the men's room just to see if she'd adorned it also, Calley chose to not move forward. Knowing Sheryl, it was likely. While she washed her hands, she stared at herself in the mirror. Sweat glistened across her forehead. "You really add extra poundage for a good workout. Don't you?" She stared down at her protruding belly.

Her heart leapt into her throat when her mother walked in. There was no means of escape from her mother's evil stare.

"Did Matthew and Lydia get off all right?" If she kept the subject on the wedding, maybe they wouldn't get into an argument.

"They got off fine. Two good people. Anyone would be proud to call them family." Her voice was curt. "I want to talk to you."

"What is it?" Calley leaned one hand on the sink, the other on her back. Better to get this done with in here, than out where everyone can see.

"I want you to consider Newman's offer to take that kid off your hands."

"I'm not giving my son to some stuffed-shirt, old man."

"I will not have you embarrass me any further than you already have. It would have been better if that child had been the one to die instead of your friend."

"How can you be so mean?" Calley's throat constricted. "This is your grandchild you're talking about."

"It will never be my grandchild. And if you don't give that kid up, I'll never speak to you again."

"That's the best news I've had all day. Now leave me alone." Calley walked around her mother, intent on returning to the reception, but her mother grabbed her arm.

"I will not leave you alone. This affects me and your sister as well."

"No, it doesn't." Calley fought tears. This was not the place for this. She came from the room with her mom following. "You want nothing to do with this baby. That's fine." Calley kept her voice low. "But don't decide later on down the line you want to play grandma because it will not happen."

"What's going on?" BJ stepped up to Calley. "Are you all right? You look pale."

"This is really none of your business," Mom said.

Rage boiled over in Calley. "It's more her business than it is yours. She's been more a mother to me, and a grandmother to this child than you'll ever be."

Mom narrowed her eyes. "You'll be sorry if you don't do what I say." She sauntered toward her table, placing a smile on her face as if nothing had happened.

How could her mother be such a hateful woman? Calley worked to catch her breath. She had to calm down, if for nothing else, the baby. She gripped BJ's hands as stars danced in front of her eyes. Calley's purse fell from her hand, scattering the contents.

Everything in front of her blurred.

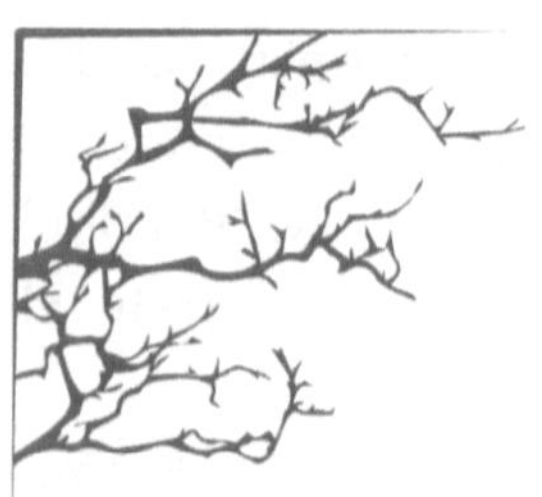

12

Riley had no choice. He had to dance with Marylou. He trudged over to her table. If he imagined Calley in his arms, he might make it through.

"Marylou…" There was a scene over by the restrooms.

"Calley!" someone yelled.

He turned. BJ had Calley by the arm, holding her up. He rushed over and caught Calley before she hit the floor.

"What happened?" He scooped her into his arms and took her to a chair.

"I don't know." BJ's voice quivered. "I think she got into an altercation with her mother. As they walked from the restroom, Calley stumbled."

Riley glanced over at Nanette. She remained seated, not even looking in their direction. He caught Allison's eye. She stood and rushed over.

"Is she all right?" Allison said. "Maybe we should take her to the emergency room."

"I'm fine. I just got dizzy." Calley wiped a trembling hand over her forehead. "I'm not sure why."

"Too much stress. The doctor said you needed to take it easy." BJ put an arm around her.

"BJ might be right," Riley said. "But I agree with Allison. We need to get you to a doctor."

"I don't want to go to the emergency room. I'll call my OB-GYN and see if she can see me. She's open on Saturdays." Calley glanced around. "Where's my purse?"

"I see it." Allison rushed to the multi-colored bag on the floor and shoved the items inside. She handed Calley her cell phone, and BJ took the purse. "Here."

Calley's fingers didn't just tremble, her entire hand shook.

Riley knew this was more than a bad bite of chicken. "Let me do it." He took the phone from her to dial. "Dr. Mason, correct?"

"Yeah." Her voice was weak.

Riley contacted the office, and Dr. Mason agreed to see Calley within the hour. Riley looked for Marylou and apologized for having to leave. He walked Calley to his car, insisting on driving her. She was certainly in no condition to drive herself. As they pulled out of the parking lot of the church, he took hold of Calley's trembling hand.

As much as he hated to dance with Marylou, he'd rather be doing that instead of rushing Calley to the doctor. He would do just about anything if it meant Calley and the baby were safe.

A CHILL RAN OVER CALLEY as she sat in the waiting room. Why had she gotten dizzy? She'd had arguments with her mother before. She glanced at two other women who waited. They each had wedding rings on their fingers. Calley covered her left hand with her right.

"What's wrong?" Riley took her hand in his.

"Just cold."

He pulled his suit jacket off and placed it around her shoulders. "Don't worry. I'm sure everything will be fine."

"I hope so." She fought tears, wanting to form. "I'm sorry you're missing the rest of the reception. You can go back if you'd like. I can call when I get done."

"No. In fact, I owe you one."

"Why?"

"If you hadn't pulled this stunt, I'd be dancing with Marylou. She'd probably be coming up with more okra recipes to tempt me into her web."

Calley laughed. "You keep making jokes like that, and people will think I'm a bad influence on you."

He wrapped his arm around her shoulder and pulled her into a hug. "That you are Calley Regan. That you are."

She was glad Lydia and Matthew had left before she got light-headed, or they might have come along. At least BJ and Sheryl were keeping things going at the reception.

Calley leaned into Riley's arm. Her body filled with warmth from being so near him. Better yet, she felt safe and assured, like everything would be all right. She rested her head against his shoulder and looked around the room. There were small signs about the defects smoking can cause on a baby if you smoke while pregnant. Another about alcohol. And one for adoption services. She shuddered as she recalled James Newman approaching her at the reception.

She turned her head toward Riley's chest, inhaling his woodsy cologne. He kissed her forehead, and a secure feeling rushed through her.

"Ms. Regan." A nurse walked through a closed door to the back room. "The doctor will see you now."

Calley's legs wobbled. She glanced down at Riley. "Would you come, too?"

Riley rose and held his hand on her back to guide her. It gave her some comfort just in case something happened to the baby.

The nurse directed her to an empty room and had her lay upon the table and placed a black blood pressure band around Calley's arm, then took her pulse and temperature. Every bad thought Calley could imagine rushed through her mind. After waiting less than ten minutes, Dr. Mason walked in. She was a tall, thin woman with deep red hair. She glanced over at Riley and nodded her head.

"I understand you had a dizzy spell." She placed a stethoscope over Calley's heart then moved to her belly.

"Yeah. I'm worried because I had a mild heart attack not too long ago."

The doctor paused and opened the file. She nodded as she read. "There was a lot of stress that day. What about today? Anything stressful?"

"Nothing much," Calley said. "I got into a fight with my mom, but that's a pretty common occurrence."

"Were you doing anything strenuous before?" The doctor wrote as she talked.

"She was dancing." Riley stepped forward from the corner of the room.

"Dancing?" The doctor snickered. "Well, the baby sounds fine. Strong heartbeat."

"Good." Calley let out a heavy breath.

"I don't think it was your heart this time, but I am worried about your blood pressure. It's extremely high. We're going to keep you here for a little while to see if we can get it down. That's probably what caused the dizzy spell. Being pregnant gives added stress to your system. Keep the dancing to a minimum. Maybe one or two at a time, then rest in between. No jumping around." She patted Calley's arm, then left.

"I guess I caused some of this." Riley walked over.

"It wasn't like I complained any. I was having fun. I should have known I was overdoing it." She adjusted the pillow behind her head. "She said I'd be here a while, so if you want to go back, I'll be here waiting."

"Not a chance." He brushed her hair from her forehead. "I'm here for the long haul, but I need to call BJ."

"I guess I need to relax more." She grinned. "Not that I'm overworked the way BJ spoils me."

"You've had a rough couple of months."

"I guess so."

"But I know the perfect way to get you to relax. You can just sit back and think of nothing."

"Really. What's that?"

"Bright and early tomorrow morning." He flicked an index finger over her nose. "I'm taking you fishing."

THE LIGHT FROM THE living room came in under Calley's bedroom door. She glanced at the digital clock on her bedside table. 1:26. All was quiet. Maybe someone forgot to turn off the light. She crept from bed and out to the living room. Riley stood against the fireplace. His t-shirt was untucked over a dark pair of sweatpants. He ran a hand over his eyes as he stared at a picture.

"Riley?"

He sniffled and wiped at his face. "Calley. I'm sorry. Did I wake you?" His voice was fragile.

"No." She took a step into the living room. "Are you all right?"

"I'm fine." He laid the picture on the mantle, walked into the kitchen, pulled out a glass, and filled it with tap water.

Calley went over to the fireplace and picked up the worn photograph. The aroma of old ash from the fireplace pit drifted over her. She swallowed hard when she saw the blonde woman in the picture holding hands with a younger, smiling Riley.

"She's very pretty," Calley said.

"Yeah. She was."

She placed the picture back down. "Were you close?"

"Yeah."

"Her name's Beth, isn't it?"

He turned and looked at her. The light from the living room cast a shadow over his tall, masculine features. "How did you know about Beth?"

"I heard you a couple of nights ago call out her name while you were sleeping." Calley walked into the dining room but kept her eyes on Riley. "Can I ask you what happened?"

"She died in a bank robbery."

Her heart leapt into her throat. "I'm so sorry. That must have been very hard for you."

He continued to stare at her.

"If you want to talk about it," she said. "I'm willing to listen."

"Thanks. There isn't much else to say. It was a while ago."

"It's obvious you still care about her very much."

He nodded. "But there comes a time when you need to move on." He let out a heavy breath. "I think we both need to get to bed if we're going fishing tomorrow."

"I thought you were kidding."

"No. The doctor said you needed to take it easy, and there's nothing more relaxing than fishing."

"I'm thinking getting up at five isn't going to be too relaxing."

"You can handle it." He gave her a weak smile.

She sighed. "Why do I get the feeling you're going to enjoy this more than I will?"

She turned and walked back to her room. The pain in Riley's face was evident. Her heart broke for him. He must have loved Beth very much. An ache filled Calley's soul. How could she be jealous of a dead woman?

RILEY RECLINED IN THE boat, his hat covering his eyes. Calley sat beside him, a fishing pole in her hand as she stared at the water. She rested her chin on her free hand. The air was warm, and the fish weren't biting.

"This is all there is to fishing?" Calley heaved a heavy breath.

"Yep."

"You just sit here and wait?"

"Yep." A smile tugged at his lips. He hadn't realized how much he missed fishing until they got out there. The horizon slowly released its hold on the sun. No breeze blew, and the surface of the lake lay flat and steady. After a hard week at work, he finally relaxed. For someone as energetic as Calley, it was probably trying on her nerves.

He'd hated Calley seeing him so vulnerable the night before. So far, she hadn't brought it up.

"There's got to be some way to spice it up and make it more fun," Calley said.

"Nothing you can do until you get a fish to take the bait."

"It's been almost an hour and a half. I don't think that's going to happen."

He rose to a seated position. "You really have no patience, do you?"

"I'm bored." She glanced around. "Well, I guess we're just going to have to talk." She looked over at Riley and gave him a big grin. "Something men just love to do."

"Why didn't you bring a book or something to keep you busy?"

"I thought there would be more to it than this. I've never been fishing before." She sighed. "It must be a man thing."

"What? Sitting back, relaxing and enjoying the view?" He swept his hand toward the open lake. When she said nothing, he figured the talking part might not be such a bad thing. There was a lot he still didn't know about her. "Okay, what do you want to talk about?"

"I don't know. Do my version of twenty questions."

"And how do you play your game of twenty questions?" He removed his hat and wiped his forehead. Not exactly what he had in mind, but why not?

"We ask each other twenty questions. It can be about anything, and the other person has to answer."

Riley shrugged his right shoulder. "Okay, ask away."

She had a serious look in her eye. One that showed concern. "Were you married to Beth?"

"Engaged."

Calley winced.

"It's okay," he said. "I don't mind talking about her. I think the wedding just brought up the memories."

"I am sorry."

Thanks." He scanned the blue water. "Now it's my turn. Where's your dad?"

"He's dead. Where are...?"

"Wait. That's it. No explanation? How am I supposed to get any information if all I get is a two-word answer?"

"You can make that your next question." She nudged his knee with her hand. "It's my turn. Where are your parents? See. You've got to word it just right, so you get as much knowledge as possible."

Riley scratched his chin. Two could play at this game. "They're dead."

"I keep hitting sore points."

"No, you don't. I'll answer anything you want me to. Of course, now it's my turn. Were you and your father close?"

"No." She swallowed hard. "I guess this isn't as much fun as I thought it would be. Is it?"

He shook his head. Calley jiggled the pole and looked out over the water.

"Let me check your bait. It must be water-logged by now." Riley hated to see the pain in Calley's eyes when she spoke about her father.

Riley leaned forward in the boat while Calley reeled the line in. She grimaced while she watched him mess with all the hooks attached to the lure.

"Ick," she said. "I'd hate to get stuck on that thing."

Riley turned the line into the water. "So, you want to talk about it? Your dad?"

She shrugged. "Do you want to talk about your parents?"

"Not much to talk about. They died in a car accident when I was eleven. My younger brother was shipped off to family in California on my father's side. I was sent to Atlanta to live with BJ, my aunt on my mother's side."

Calley stared over at him, was silent for a second, then burst into a laugh. "Do you realize you practically told me your whole childhood in about five sentences?"

"Not much of a storyteller, I guess. I'll make you a deal. If you tell me your story in five sentences or less, I promise to clean any fish you catch."

"That would be more of a threat if we actually caught any." Calley sucked in a deep breath. "Okay, here goes. My parents hated me. My sister was and still is perfect." She counted off the sentences as she went. "I ran away from home when I was sixteen and moved in with a neighbor so I could finish high school. That's about it. And you get to clean the fish."

"Why do you think your parents hated you?"

"They never believed me when I'd tell them something." A dark cloud fell over Calley's expression. Pain flashed into her eyes. Before he could ask her anything further, the pole tugged up and down.

"What's happening?" Calley jerked up the rod.

"I think you've got something." He placed his arm around her, helping her reel in the fish. "Here, guide it in. Not too quick or you'll lose him. That's it, nice and steady."

Calley spun the reel, moving the pole as instructed. She gasped when a fish sprang out of the water.

"He's a good-sized trout." Riley pulled out the net and placed it in the water under fish. "I'd say he's about sixteen to eighteen pounds."

Riley held up the flopping fish for Calley to see.

She bounced away when he got close to her. The boat swayed back and forth. "It's all fishy smelling."

He laughed. "I guess that's because he's a fish." He jerked the net toward her. "Come on, touch him. He feels fishy, too. Nice and slimy."

"Stop it. I'm going to tell your aunt on you." She giggled and moved back to the seat behind the one she was on.

Riley got up on one knee and shook the fish in front of her face, laughing. Calley wrenched to one side, and the boat lurched. The net fell, and Riley slipped. He couldn't catch his balance. His feet skated as his boots slid. With nothing to grab hold of, he flipped over the side of the boat into the water.

"Are you all right?" Calley said once his head popped out of the water. He coughed out some water from his lungs.

She stared down at him. The sun behind her cast a glow of yellow over her hair. Man, she was pretty.

"Yeah, just didn't expect it. But it feels good in this heat." He splashed water up at her. "Why don't you join me?"

"Two reasons. First, there are fish in that water. And the second, I'd sink to the bottom with this belly of mine."

"Suffer in the heat then." He dove back under. He'd tip the boat to send her in but wasn't sure how well she could swim, even when not pregnant.

He came up again and tugged his boots off. After draining them of water, he tossed them and his hat into the boat.

"Just like my bait, you're going to get water-logged," Calley said.

"Then I'll climb back up and shake on you like an old wet dog."

He ducked back under the water. His goal was to head under the boat to the other side. When he opened his eyes underwater to get his bearings, the air he had in his lungs expelled.

Before him was a bloated body.

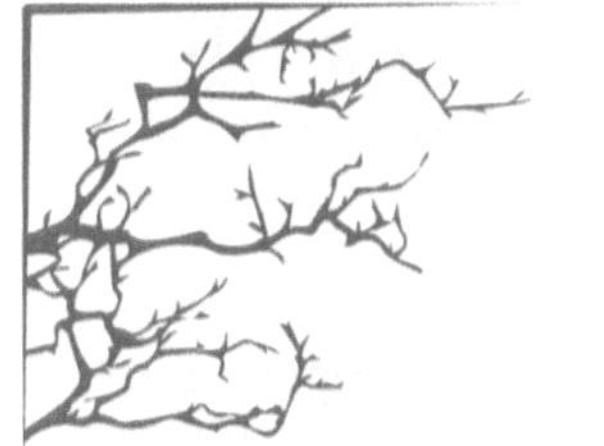

13

Riley's heart had finally returned to its normal rhythm. Who'd have thought they'd find a body in that lake? He watched as two divers from the Catoosa County Sheriff's Department entered the water. They would check for identification before they brought the body up. Riley hadn't recognized the man, but he didn't stick around very long to get a closer look. The man's eyes were wide opened, and tape covered his mouth. Definitely not an accident.

He glanced over at Calley sitting on a log looking out at the water. Maybe he should have taken her back to the house. It wasn't like the body was going anywhere. She glanced at him and gave him a quick smile.

It had begun as a wonderful day, one with sunshine, a rod in his hand, and a wonderful woman beside him. He was glad he'd been there when Calley caught her first fish. It was a memory she'd never forget. And he'd had fun teasing her with the trout. He couldn't recall the last time he'd laughed so hard.

"Riley," Deputy Green called out to him. "They say it'll be about five minutes. They couldn't find anything to ID him, but they'll look further once they get him up."

Riley walked over to Calley. "How are you holding up?"

"So far, so good. At least there's some action." She used her hand to block the sun from her eyes. "Much better than just sitting and waiting for fish to bite."

He sat down on the log next to her. "I'm sorry this ruined our day."

"What ruined? I just wish I'd had a camera for when you came up out of that water. You would've thought Jaws was after you."

119

Riley laughed. He imagined he looked funny, choking, and hacking out of the water. Finding a dead man would be enough to send a shock through just about anyone.

"You practically walked on water getting back in that boat. There for a minute, I thought you were Jesus returning." She nudged him with her shoulder. "I bet you keep your eyes closed from here on in when you go swimming. Huh?"

"Probably." He wrapped an arm around her and pulled her to him. He kissed her on the forehead. "I'm glad you came with me this morning. I had fun."

"Can I quote you on that?" Her hazel eyes shined in the sun.

Deputy Green waved in their direction and yelled, "They're bringing him up now."

"Would you like to sit in the car while they're bringing him up?"

"No. I can't see him that well from here. So, I think I'll be fine."

"Are you sure you're not too hot?" He looked back at Calley, his arm still around her. If so many people weren't around, he'd be even more tempted to kiss her wonderfully full pink lips.

"Would you quit mothering me? I'm fine." She sniffed the air. "You smell like fish."

"I imagine I do."

"More like lake and fish combination."

"You're a pain. You know that?" He took his hat off and placed it on her head. "This'll keep some of the sun off you." It fell to her eyes. "We need to get you one that fits."

"I kind of like yours."

"But I can't see you."

"But I can see you. That's more important." She adjusted the hat back on her head. "Besides, if you can't see my face, I can be thinking anything, and you'd never know it."

"You don't need to keep any secrets from me." Riley's voice was low as he looked out at the divers swimming over to the boat. They were towing the body with them. "I'm going to take you home once they get him up. I'll be busy the rest of the day."

"Hey! Wait a minute. You're supposed to clean my fish." She shook her head. "Let me guess, I'm going to have to clean it? Well, let me tell you, mister, I don't know how. So there."

"I'll keep it in the pail and get to it when I get home. Unless BJ does it first."

"I can't believe you're welching on our bet."

"I rather be home cleaning the fish." He then added in a whisper. "With you."

She wrapped her arm around his bicep. He removed the hat from her head when it bumped his arm. She leaned her chin against him and stared up into his eyes.

She was so pretty. He kissed her forehead and returned his attention back to the dive boat. He needed to keep focused on the pending investigation. As much as he hated to.

Divers pulled the body from the water. Even from a distance, Riley could see the body was bloated. The man would be almost unrecognizable. Hopefully, the morgue could get his prints, and they'd be in AFIS.

"Well, I guess I'd better get you home so I can head over to the M.E.'s office." He rose and held out his hand for Calley.

Her face was a deathly white.

CALLEY FOUGHT THE URGE to vomit. Why didn't she insist on going back to the house? She could have walked or called BJ.

"Are you all right?" Riley pulled her to her feet. "Don't look at it." He tugged her into him. "I should have taken you home before they pulled him up. I'm sorry."

She burrowed deeper in his arms. She swallowed back bile rising in her throat. "It's okay." Her voice was weak. "I'm going to be fine."

"Take in a deep breath." Riley reached down into the bag he'd brought and pulled out some water. "Here, take a drink."

She did as instructed. Her eyes diverted to the sand, so she wasn't tempted to look at the water.

Riley guided her to the car. She barely heard him as he hollered to someone to let them know he was taking her to the house. The ride back was a blur. She couldn't remember him helping her from the car. They walked into the house, and she headed directly to the bathroom and got sick.

"There, there. Lean on me. It must have been a horrific sight." BJ helped her to the bed.

Calley crawled under the covers. Her whole body trembled.

"I can't believe that nephew of mine." BJ shook her head. "He should have brought you directly home. The last thing you need is this stress. Tsk."

"It wasn't his fault." Her voice shook. "He didn't know."

"Well, I'm going to fix you some soup. You just lay here. Try to get your mind off it."

"Where's Riley?"

"He had to go back to the lake. But don't you worry about him none. He's dealt with stuff like this before when he worked in Atlanta." She patted Calley's back. "He'll be home later."

Tears fell down Calley's face. There was no way she could get her mind off it. When she closed her eyes, she saw the body. The blue Polo shirt and khaki pants. And she knew.

Someone had killed Peter.

14

Calley reclined on the bed, her pillow wet from tears. Why couldn't she say anything? Why didn't she tell Riley she recognized the man's clothing? Maybe it was the shock of seeing the body pulled from the water. Or maybe it was because she didn't want Riley to know what type of person she really was.

"Child, how are you feeling?" BJ came in and sat down beside her. "I've a good mind to call up that boy and let him have it with both barrels."

Calley sat up and wiped her face. Her hands still smelt like fish. She wasn't sure why. All she did was sit in the boat and hold on to the pole. "It wasn't his fault. I told him I was fine. I didn't know it would be..." She swallowed back the bile rising in her throat.

"He still should have brought you home."

"I wish he had. Then I wouldn't have seen him." Calley sniffled.

"I'm sure it was a shock. Even the most seasoned officer would have a hard time with something like that." BJ rose from the bed. "I've got some soup on the stove. Would you like me to bring it to you?"

"No. I'll get up." Calley swung her legs around the side of the bed. She plodded to the bathroom to wash her hands and face. The mirror showed a reflection of blotched cheeks. She had every right to cry. At one time, she thought she loved Peter.

A knock sounded on the bathroom door. "What would you like to drink?"

"Tea will be fine." She shuffled into the dining room and dropped into a chair. She needed to call Riley and tell him she recognized the clothing on the body. A sob stopped in her throat. The sooner he knew it was Peter, the sooner he could find the person responsible. She glanced around.

"What are you looking for, child?" BJ patted Calley on the shoulder, then sat down beside her.

"My phone."

"You don't need to make any calls right now. You need to relax. For both yours and the baby's sake."

"You don't understand. I knew him."

"You knew who, dear?"

"The man in the water. It was Peter."

RILEY GLANCED OVER the preliminary report on the body. This is definitely not the way he'd hoped his Sunday would end when it first started. The man had a hole in his chest from a bullet wound, but he needed to know what caliber. His cell rang. BJ. She would have to wait. He knew Calley was in good hands as long as she was with BJ. And the last thing he needed at that moment was her scolding him for keeping Calley at a crime scene.

Deputy Green stuck his head in the door. "We got an I.D."

"Who is he?"

"Some guy named Peter Jameson. From Atlanta."

Riley swallowed hard. Could this guy be associated with the woman following Calley? "He have any priors?"

"Nothing. I looked on-line, and he's an attorney and has one of those social media pages." Green paused. "Take a look."

Riley walked out to Green's desk. Peter Jameson had a very professional appearance with a nice suit and tie. His status on the website claimed he was single and had his own business, making six figures a year. There were several photographs of him sailing and water skiing. Riley clicked on Jameson's friends' pictures. Several women, all beautiful. Then Riley's heart dropped to his stomach. In one photo, Jameson held his arm around Calley.

"Man." He had no choice. She's currently the only connection he had to the dead man other than the wife.

"What do you want me to do?" Green's voice went quiet. "I can forget I saw it."

"We don't hide evidence just to protect people we know." He slammed the chair under the desk. "Get over to my house and pick her up."

"What should I tell her I'm bringing her in for?"

"She's being questioned about Peter Jameson's murder."

CALLEY'S HANDS TREMBLED. Maybe she was mistaken. That type of clothing was popular among professional men. BJ tried to call Riley, but when she didn't answer, she suggested they wait until he came home to tell him of her suspicions. Between the heat and the shock of the bloated body, Calley could be wrong. She jumped at the sound of someone at the front door.

"I'll get it." BJ patted Calley's hand before answering. "Why, Vincent, how are you?"

"I'm doing okay, I guess." Deputy Green scraped his feet on the welcome mat.

"And how's your mother?"

"Fine." He removed his hat before entering. He glanced over at Calley, then looked away. "I've come to take Ms. Regan to the station."

"Me? Why?" Calley's mouth went dry.

"What are you talking about, taking her to the station?" BJ stood between the deputy and Calley. "You know full well she's very pregnant, and she doesn't need this type of stress."

"I've been asked to." He stared at the floor. "The sheriff said to come get ya. It's about the man in the lake. His name was Peter Jameson."

"We know," BJ said. "I tried to reach Riley."

Calley's heart pounded in her ears. She tried to calm herself, for the baby's sake.

"The sheriff also said to get her gun."

"Her gun? Just what in Sam Hill is going on here?" BJ placed her hands on her hips. "You just stay right there while I call that nephew of mine."

Calley caught BJ by the arm. "It's okay." She looked at Deputy Green, who had yet to raise his eyes to look at either woman. "The gun's in my purse."

He walked over and unclasped it. He removed her tan wallet and lifted the colorful purse and shook it around. "I don't see it."

Calley's skin crawled. She rushed over and dug through the bag. It wasn't there. *Think. Where could it be?* "The wedding. My purse fell at the wedding. A bunch of stuff fell out."

"I can vouch for that," BJ said. "I recall seeing the purse lying on the floor. The insides were scattered all over."

Her heart sank. *This can't be happening. Why wasn't the gun returned, or at the very least given it to Riley?* "Maybe it's still at the church." She looked up at Deputy Green. He wasn't as good looking as Riley, but not bad in his own way. Blondish red hair and freckles on his face told of his Irish heritage.

"Let me make a call." He walked out the front door to the porch.

Calley couldn't take her eyes off his back. *Please, please let them find the gun.*

Deputy Green returned inside. "They're heading over to the church to see if they can locate it. The sheriff said to bring you in."

"Am I under arrest?" Calley's lip trembled.

"I think he just wants to ask you some questions."

"Why can't he ask her here?" BJ's jaw tightened.

"I'm not sure, ma'am." Deputy Green hung his head. "I just know he wants to talk about the murder."

Calley's heart stopped. Murder? How could Riley think she had anything to do with Peter's death?

RILEY STARED OUT THE window at the woods. Daylight faded as the sun floated into the horizon. Could this man be the person who attacked Calley in Atlanta? If so, why didn't she just name him? After all, he killed her friend. A knock drew him from his thoughts. He turned and saw a pained expression on Calley's face. He had no other choice. This was his job. A man had been killed. He needed honest answers, and if putting her in jail got them, he'd do it.

Wouldn't he?

"Have a seat." He gestured toward a chair on the other side of his desk.

She didn't say a word as she walked in. Once seated, she looked up at him, her eyes sad and scared. "Did they find my gun at the church?"

"No." He let out a weighted breath and sat down. "We've got a call into Atlanta to compare the bullets you shot at your place with the one in the body." Calley grimaced at his words. Riley tried not to notice he was the person causing her distress. "The man in the water was Peter Jameson."

"I know."

Her admission startled him. "What do you mean, you know?"

"I recognized the clothing. Besides, Deputy Green told us." She looked down at her lap while she spoke. "Peter came by the house about a week ago."

Riley wiped a hand down his face. "Why didn't you tell me?"

"I didn't really see any need. He said he was just checking on me."

"You're the only connection I have to this man."

"No." She shook her head. "His wife was here. Remember, you stopped her." Tears grew in her eyes.

"I remember." He looked down at his desk filled with papers he'd rather be working on than doing what he was doing. "I also remember you said you never heard of her."

CALLEY EXPECTED YELLING or some form of anger, but all she got was silence. Riley's eyes hardened, and his lips tightened. How could he think she did this? She'd never hurt anyone, not even Peter.

She glanced around his office. It was the first time she'd seen it. As with everything in his life, it was neatly organized with a few files on his desk and one painting over a credenza which held a neat stack of books behind him. The seconds became minutes. It would be better if he yelled and got it over with.

"Do you really think I killed him?" She broke the silence.

"I don't know. You tell me." He glared at her. "Who was he?"

"A guy I used to date. I didn't know at the time he was married."

"That gives you a motive."

"It also gives his wife one."

"It isn't her gun missing."

Calley swallowed back her fear. There was no way this was happening. "How do we know it was my gun? You can't be sure. Besides, anyone from the wedding could have it. The contents of my purse fell all over the floor."

"Why were you carrying a gun in the first place?"

"Peter's wife came up to me in a store. She made it clear she knew how to deal with women like me." Calley stared at her lap. "I got scared. So I bought a gun and learned how to use it."

"We won't know if it is your gun until we hear from Atlanta. It's just too much of a coincidence. I have a dead man you knew, and this is the first time I've heard about a missing gun."

She darted out of the chair. "I didn't know it was missing. It's not like I look at it every day. The wedding was just yesterday."

"You should have." He slammed his hand on the desk, which made her flinch. "If you're going to carry around a gun, you need to know where it is at all times." He rose and faced her. "A man's been killed, and a .38 was used. I believe that's the caliber of gun you own."

"I'm sure a lot of people own a .38." Her mind swirled with other possibilities.

"Yeah, but a lot of people don't know the victim."

He tossed a photograph at her. She looked at it and almost fainted. Peter. Only he wasn't the handsome man she remembered. His skin was yellowish, and his lips were blue. She lowered herself back into the chair.

"You should have told me who you thought it was at the lake."

"I couldn't. I must have been in shock or something." She shouldn't have lied about knowing him in the beginning.

"Certain things come too easy for you, but shock isn't one of them."

"What's that supposed to mean?" Anger grew inside.

He walked around and placed one hand on the desk and another on her chair. She swallowed hard again, and her breathing intensified.

His jaw tightened as he said, "Like lying and keeping secrets."

She bolted up again and faced him. "I didn't lie. And I'd never met Mrs. Jameson that morning I left. She accosted me in Lou's grocery."

"Another secret."

"I saw no need to tell you. I didn't feel it was important to let you know I had an affair with a married man." Tears stood at attention in her eyes.

"I never called you a tramp."

"But you think it," she blurted. "Anyone would. It's bad enough I'm pregnant and not married, but pregnant by a married man. That's even worse."

Riley's shoulders straightened. He took a step back, his eyes wide open from the shock of her statement. "Peter Jameson is the father of your baby?"

RILEY'S GUT ACHED AS he stared at Calley. This was a nightmare. She dropped back into the chair. Why couldn't she have kept that part a secret? He walked back behind his desk and answered the buzzing phone.

"Yeah, Silvi."

"We got the preliminary police report from Atlanta. They say the bullet from the body matched one taken from the wall in Calley's apartment."

Riley sucked in a deep breath and sat down and looked at Calley. "Where's the gun?" His voice came out low.

"I don't know. It was in my purse." She held the arms of the chair, her knuckles white. "You can't think I did this."

"It doesn't matter what I think. You have motive, means, and opportunity. That's all we need." He turned away, refusing to look up at her. It would only tear his heart apart more.

"I had no reason to kill Peter."

"He was the father of your child. Maybe you had a fight. He didn't want it or, worse, he wanted full custody. The man's a lawyer. He would have a good chance of getting what he wanted."

"No." Her voice quivered.

"The bullet came from your gun."

A loud breath escaped her, and she covered her mouth with her hand. Tears fell from her eyes. "Is everything so black and white with you? Listen to that voice inside. The one telling you I didn't do this." She sobbed. "You've got to believe me."

If someone was setting her up, they were doing a fairly good job at it. He didn't want to believe it, but everything pointed to her. Besides, why would someone want her out of the way? None of this made sense. Maybe he should never have let his heart get involved with this woman. But he had, and now he was about to pay the price. He pulled up the phone.

"Silvi, come in here." He walked to the window. Calley's sobs echoed in his soul. There was only one thing he could do.

When Silvi opened the door, Riley didn't bother to turn around. He ran a hand over his face and said, "Book her."

15

Calley followed Silvi down the hallway to a small room. A machine for taking pictures stood on one side. A long table with assorted boxes and files were on the other wall.

"None of this will hurt," Silvi said.

"Not physically anyway." Calley turned to the door, hoping Riley would walk in and stop this. Maybe it was his idea of a prank. If he'd stop it right now, she'd laugh, though she didn't find any of it funny. She just wanted out of there.

"Come over here and stand on this mark." Silvi pointed to an X on the floor. Calley did as instructed. Silvi walked behind the camera. "Look at the red spot." Calley startled at the blinding flash.

"Now this way." She guided Calley by her elbow to the long table. "This will wash off." She placed Calley's fingers in an ink pad, then on a piece of paper on at a time. Silvi gave Calley a wipe to remove the ink from her hands once they were finished.

"Right this way."

Silvi directed Calley out the door to the back. A buzzer sounded as they approached a large steel door. It slid to the right. They walked through, and it slammed shut. Calley jumped and looked over her shoulder at the closed door. She wanted to run, but there was no way out. Another buzzer sounded, opening up the bars in front of them. Calley paused. Her feet didn't want to move.

"Please. Don't make me," she cried.

Silvi's hand directed her forward. "It's all right. Most people get scared when they first come back here. Don't worry. There's no one else here but you."

132

The bars shut behind Calley. There were six cages in total, three on each side. Silvi led her to the second one on the right. The cell held two cots on opposite sides and a stainless-steel toilet connected to the back wall. Calley walked through the opened cell door. The bars slammed shut behind her. Her legs barely carried her to one of two cots. She glanced at everything. How did she get herself into this mess? Tears rolled down her cheeks. Her fear no longer allowed her to contain them.

RILEY RUBBED HIS EYES. His office sofa wasn't near as comfortable as his bed. He couldn't leave until he found something to clear Calley. BJ had called several times, but he refused to answer his phone. When she showed up at the sheriff's department door the night before, he refused her access to the building. It wouldn't surprise him to find out she spent the night in the parking lot.

Just after eight o'clock in the morning, the medical examiner phoned with the conclusion of the autopsy. Peter Jameson died from asphyxiation. There was water in his lungs. He had been alive when someone tossed into the lake. His taped hands were behind his back. Whoever killed him tied his ankles to a cinderblock. It would have been smarter to toss his body in the Chattahoochee-Oconee National Forest not too far away. Would Calley have been callous enough to kill someone in this way? Riley knew the answer was a resounding no. And she wouldn't have been strong enough with her pregnancy.

Someone was after her, whether it be to harm her or to put her in prison. No matter the evidence. He was sure of it.

He got on the internet and pulled up the number to the notification department of the Atlanta Police Department. He needed someone to contact the widow.

"Sergeant, this is Sheriff Riley Owens of the Lincolnville Sheriff's Office. We have us a body up here that we've identified as Attorney Peter Jameson. We need you to notify the man's wife who lives in Atlanta and have her provide a positive ID."

"We can do that for you. Do you have an address on her?"

"Just what the license says. If you can't find her, try his office. They might know how to find her."

Riley hung up the phone and cradled his head in his hands. Once Fifi Jameson came to claim her husband's body, she'd be in his jurisdiction where he could interrogate her. But right now, she was off limits.

He thought back to the wedding. When he scooped Calley in his arms, she didn't have her purse. In fact, Allison was the one who retrieved it. Maybe she picked up the gun. For all he knew, she might have as much a reason to kill Peter as Calley did. The man was obviously a player. Pitting one sister against the other wouldn't be above a cad like that. There's also the possibility that Allison found it and gave it to her mother, Nanette. Would she know who Peter Jameson was? And if so, would she be cold blooded enough to shoot him and toss him in the lake? Nanette is obviously not happy about the baby.

He couldn't imagine either would have the strength alone. Maybe together.

Riley hadn't put that Peter Jameson was the father of Calley's baby on his report the night before. There was enough evidence already with her gun as the murder weapon. He wouldn't give the prosecutor anymore. He knew she didn't kill him. Riley needed time to prove it.

He leaned back. Two female figures heading his way caught his attention. Just what he needed — a parade. He should consider himself lucky Sheryl and Lydia were out of town. BJ stormed through his door, not bothering to knock with Allison close on her heels.

"Who do you think you are, Riley Owens, locking Calley in jail?" BJ placed her hands on her hips and stood in front of his desk. "And not answering my calls or allowing me in last night?"

"I had no choice. Her gun was used to kill the man."

"You can't possibly believe she's guilty. Can you?" BJ's voice quivered.

He glanced up. Her brow creased and her eyes were downcast. He hated to hurt his aunt like this. "It doesn't matter what I believe. It's the evidence that counts."

"But she's pregnant," Allison said.

"A lot of pregnant women end up in prison." He paused. "By the way, at the wedding, when you scooped up Calley's purse, did you find her gun?"

"Gun? No. I didn't know she had one. There was her wallet, her keys, assorted odds and ends." Allison took a step forward. "This means she didn't have it. Someone else did. Right?"

"It could mean that. Or it could mean she lied and had the gun somewhere else at the time of the wedding so she could be ready to kill Peter Jameson." Riley hoped for a reaction from Allison but only saw concern. "She was at the hospital and then home."

"That's the only saving grace for her, but that doesn't mean she didn't sneak out."

Riley recalled his talk with Calley that evening. Was she planning to leave when she came into the living room?

No, she was dressed for bed, not a midnight excursion.

She was innocent. He knew it but didn't dare let on that he believed in her. Someone might show up with more evidence against her. Then he'd know who to go after.

"I want to see my sister." Allison stood in the doorway, tears in her eyes. "Please."

Riley pressed the intercom on his phone. "Silvi, take these two back to the meeting room. Bring Calley in to see them." When he hung up, he said, "You have five minutes."

"I'll take as long as I desire, young man." BJ gave him a stern nod.

Allison paused before walking out the door. "We've got to help her."

Riley ran his hand through his hair. "Everything right now is against her."

They walked through the side door leading to the meeting room. He let out a heavy sigh, got up, and trudged to the window. He glanced up at the blue sky. It was a beautiful day. Too nice to be sitting in a cell.

"Please God, let my best be good enough this time."

CALLEY HESITATED IN the hallway, afraid of whom she might find on the other side of that door. When she walked in, BJ and Alliston stood inside. Mascara tracks led from Allison's eyes. BJ's jaw clenched. They looked wonderful to Calley. She let out a breath of air she'd been holding, and a grin came over her face.

"What are you ladies doing in a place like this? Come to see my new digs?" She laughed but felt no humor behind it.

"Are you all right?" BJ rushed up and gave her a hug. The concern in BJ's eyes made warmth tug at Calley's heart.

"Wonderful. I hear they're serving meatloaf for dinner."

BJ brushed back Calley's hair from her face. "I'm glad you can stay light in this situation. I'm ready to shoot Riley."

"I'd loan you my gun, but it's apparently missing." Calley didn't feel humorous. The doctor said she needed to watch her blood pressure. Joking was all she could do after a long night of crying.

BJ walked with her arm around Calley to a chair on the other side of a table in the middle of the room. She glanced around the room and stared at the mirror on the wall. "And don't anyone be listening in." BJ walked up to the mirror. "We're acting as Calley Regan's counsel, so this is a private conversation."

Calley laughed. "Let me guess, you've been watching cop shows on television?"

"No. Reading books." BJ grinned from ear to ear.

Allison sat on the opposite side of the table. "We're going to see a lawyer later. We're hoping once they get you in front of a judge, they'll let us post bail so we can get you out of here."

"You'll be out before you know it." BJ patted Calley's hand. "And don't judge that nephew of mine to harshly. He can be a real stickler for the law, but I know he's trying to find the right answer."

"I'm not too sure. He seems to think I'm guilty." Calley's heart skipped a beat at her words. He should know her better than that.

"I don't believe that for a minute. And neither should you."

"Then why'd he lock me up?" Calley hoped BJ was right, but she couldn't be sure about anything anymore. A knock on the door startled her. Silvi stuck her head back in.

"I'm sorry, but that's all the time you have." She kept her voice low.

"You keep your chin up. You'll be home soon." BJ hugged Calley before turning to the door.

Allison paused. "Can I have another minute with my sister?" Her eyes pleaded with Silvi. "Please?"

Silvi nodded and led BJ from the room.

"How's Mom doing?" Calley wasn't sure she wanted to hear how her mother felt about all this. Best to get it over with.

"She's upset. How will people think when they hear, yada, yada, yada. Made her mad when I said I was coming, but I had to make sure you were all right."

"As you can see, I'm hanging in there." She then added, "By a noose."

"Don't worry. God will take care of you." Allison stood in the middle of the room, her hands in her jacket pockets.

Calley scoffed. "God stopped taking care of me a long time ago."

"Don't say that."

"It's not His fault. I'm too much trouble for Him to mess with."

Silence fell between the two women. Allison finally spoke, her eyes directed at the floor. "I asked Mom about Uncle Joe's trial."

"I'm not really in the mood to talk about this right now." Calley moved to the corner of the room. She wanted to become one with it. To forget everything she was going through, and everything she'd been through in the past.

"She claimed you were wild for years, and that you testified against Joe just to upset the family." Allison took a step toward Calley. "I don't recall you being wild. You didn't lie. Did you?"

Calley shook her head. Talking about Uncle Joe hit a sore spot within her. She's not sure she could go into this, but her sister pressed on.

"What did he do to you?" Allison's voice lowered, and her jaw tightened.

"He tried to scare me, but only made me mad." Calley turned and looked at her sister. "We were in the back room of the garage during the Fourth of July party. He kept saying you were the pretty one, but he could make me feel special." A shiver ran up her back. "Piece of garbage. Probably figured I'd be easier because I was so much uglier than you."

"You were never ugly, Calley." Allison paused, then spoke in a whisper. "Did he rape you?"

"Rape, no. He kissed me and told me how I was going to be his special girl. Then he touched my breast."

Allison gasped.

"I kneed him in the groin and ran out." A smile came over Calley's lips as she recalled the pained expression on his face.

"Why didn't you tell anyone?"

"I did. I told both Mom and Dad. They couldn't believe good old Uncle Joe would do something like that." Calley drew her arms over her chest. "They said I must have been mistaken by his actions. But I knew there was no mistake."

Allison walked over to Calley who faced the wall. "That's when you started hating everyone."

"Not everyone, just them." Calley paused, then added, "And you."

"Why me? You never told me about Uncle Joe. I might have believed you."

"Because I told Mom and Dad the truth about things all the time, but they never believed me. My sixth-grade teacher, Ms. Goozeman, told me she hated me. When I told Mom, she just said I was just trying to get Old Lady Gooseface in trouble because I got a bad grade on a test. Mom wouldn't even look at my paper to see I should have gotten a better grade." Calley turned and faced her sister. "But you, they always believed you, even when you lied."

Allison's eyes widened.

Calley let out a laugh. "Remember when they caught you with a pack of cigarettes? You claimed they were someone else's, but I knew you were smoking. I saw you. I also know you stole those earrings when you went to the mall with Molly. But you told Mom they were given to you. She and Dad believed every word you ever said."

"Why didn't you let anyone know? You could have gotten me into trouble."

"It's not like they would have believed me if I had."

"I'm sorry you grew to hate me. I should have seen what was going on." Allison put her hand on Calley's arm. "From this point forward, I'll work at being a better big sister." She pulled Calley into a hug.

"I'm so scared." Tears formed in Calley's eyes. "How can I have a baby in prison?"

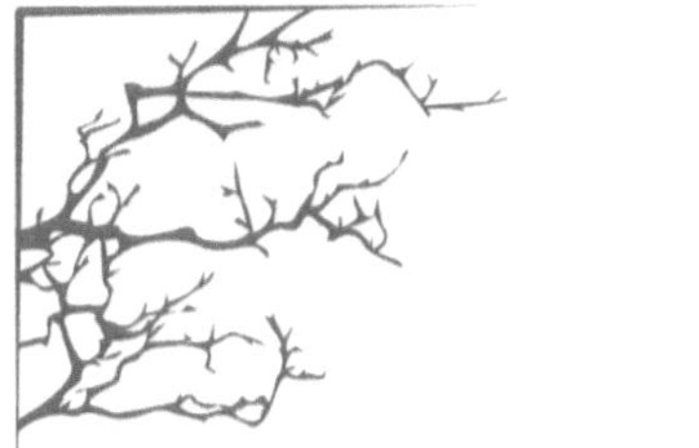

16

Riley listened to Calley speak with her friends from the other side of the two-way mirror. The molestation explained why Calley ran away when she was a teen. It also gave him someone else to look at with a motive to frame her. Calley's face looked troubled. She had good reason to be. If he didn't find someone else to pin this murder on, the prosecuting attorney would choose her.

"You've got some good friends," Silvi said to Calley in the meeting room. "BJ especially. I don't think I'd want to get on her bad side."

Riley grinned. Silvi knew he was listening in. Maybe she was giving him a warning.

"I guess I need to go back now." Calley's voice wobbled.

"Yeah. I'm sorry." Silvi held the door open for Calley. Before closing it, she shot Riley a desperate look. How was it Calley could make friends in such a short amount of time?

Riley stood for a moment, staring into the empty room. He hated the idea of questioning her about her uncle, but the more who might have reason to set her up, the better it could help Calley's case. He paused at the door before walking out.

He sucked in a deep breath and nodded for the guard to open the last door. He knew Calley would probably hate him. She should. Be hurt more than mad. He stopped just inside the cell area. She glanced over at him, then diverted her eyes to the far wall. The sorrow in her eye caused him pain.

"How are you doing?" he asked.

"I don't think you should speak to me without my attorney." Her voice was uneven. Probably trying not to cry.

How could she not understand what he was doing? He nodded to the man behind the wall at his left. The cell door clicked. It slid to the right. He walked in and sat on the cot opposite her. The mattress was thin and uncomfortable. He'd have to either double them up for Calley or find her another place to sleep.

Her hair had fallen loose from her ponytail on the back of her head and red swollen eyes only made him feel worse. Her hunched shoulders screamed of her anxiety and dark circles whispered of the lack of sleep she needed for the baby's sake and her own.

"Tell me about your Uncle Joe." His voice was low. He knew it was a subject that would upset her.

She gasped. "You were listening in on Allison and me. Weren't you?"

"The conversation wasn't privileged. Neither Allison nor BJ are your counsel. Besides, I was hoping Allison would say something to incriminate herself."

"Allison?" Calley shook her head. "She'd never hurt anyone."

"She's the one who picked up the contents of your purse."

"The only thing she'd do with it is give it to my mother. Now she'd set me up in a heartbeat."

"I'm trying to help you, Calley. I need someone else to offer to the prosecuting attorney. There's Jameson's wife, this guy who kicked your car in, and now your uncle." She glared at him. "If I don't find someone, they'll decide it was you." He paused before continuing. "When's the last time you saw your uncle?"

"At the wedding. He came with my mom."

"That's good. What's his last name? I need to check on his whereabouts. To see if he might have been in town."

"His name's Joe Mercer. I can understand him being mad at me." She turned to face Riley. "But why kill Peter? I don't think he knew him. No one in my family did."

"What was the case you testified against Mercer for?"

She breathed out a deep sigh. "He raped a fifteen-year-old while she was drunk. They asked around the family for anyone he molested, and they found me. I was more than happy to go up against him. To show him I wasn't afraid."

The words Matthew had said in the church returned to Riley. "You're one strong woman."

"Then why do I feel like I'm falling apart?" She swallowed hard, and her jaw tightened. "Does this mean you don't think I killed Peter?"

"I know you didn't."

Her mouth opened as if she was going to speak. Instead, she crossed her arms over her chest and smirked. "How can you be so sure? As you said, I have a motive."

"But you weren't the only one." Riley leaned forward on the cot. "His wife did also. And now your uncle might have, if it meant framing you and sending you to jail. Was he convicted?"

"He got seven years and had to register as a sex offender."

"Very good motive to want to hurt you."

"I still don't know how he would know about Peter. Unless he'd been watching me for a while." She shuddered. "Why did you put me in jail if you thought I was innocent?"

"I had no choice."

Her eyes locked in a forward stare. She leaned her shoulder against the nearby wall with her legs out in front of her.

"I know you didn't kill this guy, Calley. You've got to believe I have my reasons for doing everything I've done." Her jaw loosened, and she stared at him. Her expression was one of bewilderment. He continued. "What do you know about Fifi Jameson?"

She turned so her back was now against the wall, and her legs hung over the edge of the cot. "She's a hag."

"Is that because she was married to the man you were seeing, or do you have a basis for feeling that way?"

"Because of how she came up to me in Lou's." Calley shook her head. "I didn't even know Peter was married when we dated. I'd have never gone out with him if I did."

"I know."

She gave a smile that quickly faded. "If she did it, how did she get my gun?"

"I have Rayleene, the photographer from Lydia's wedding, sending me copies of the wedding pictures. It's a long shot, but we might get lucky and see someone picking up your stuff without anyone knowing it or we might see someone there who shouldn't have been." Riley rose. "I understand Allison and BJ are getting you a lawyer."

She nodded. "He doesn't do adoptions though."

"Why do you need an attorney that handles adoptions?"

"If anything happens to me, my mom will get first dibs on the baby. She'll give him off to that Newman guy. I have to make sure the baby goes to a good home." Her lip trembled and tears formed.

"I'm not going to let anything happen to you."

"How can you stop it? Even if you don't think I did it, there's enough evidence to make me sit in jail until after the baby's born. Besides, what type of mother would I be, under arrest and all?"

"I haven't officially placed you under arrest."

"Then why am I in here? Can you do that? Keep me here?" She spoke in angry panted breaths. "I thought you were Mr. Go-by-the-book. So, when it comes to me, you throw the book out the window?"

Riley waited until she was done with her rant. He sucked in a deep breath. His whole career was on the line for this woman. "It's clear someone's after you, Calley."

"What do you mean?"

"Something in my gut tells me that guy in Atlanta was after you. And now you're being set up for the murder of a guy you used to date. I figured this was the safest place for you to be right now." He knelt in front of her. "This is the only place I can be sure you'll be safe twenty-four hours a day."

"I thought this Fulbright, or whatever his name is, killed Eva."

"He got paid twenty thousand just before it happened."

The breath left her. Someone wanted her dead? That doesn't make sense. She pushed herself up from the cot and shoved around him. "Why didn't you just ask me to come to work with you if you thought I was in danger? Why lock me up? Treat me like a criminal?" She crossed her arms over her chest, and her eyes returned to the back wall.

"I'm hoping whoever this is will think you're out of the way. Someone went to a lot of trouble to set you up here in Lincolnville, and we don't know why. I'm hoping they make a mistake or take care of whatever business it is they need to." He stood behind her and placed his hands on her shoulders. "Besides, you should know me well enough to know I might have other reasons."

"How am I supposed to know that?" She shoved his arms off and moved away from him. "Men. They get mad when women play games and don't say what's bothering them. Yet they think women can read their minds." She shook her head.

"How can you not know after these last few months?"

She turned to face him. "What am I supposed to know? That you put me in jail to protect me?"

"I'm not much for words. Do I have to spell it out for you, Calley?"

"Spell what out? Just say what you mean."

He placed his hands on the side of her face and bent down. His lips touched hers, first soft, then firm. He brought his hands around her waist and pulled her to him. After the kiss, he stared into her eyes. "Did I make myself clear?"

"Uh-huh," her voice squeaked.

Riley's phone buzzed in his pocket. "I've got to take this."

He finished his conversation and hung up. "It seems Mrs. Jameson's in town. She's been staying in a rental on the west side of town for over a month. I'm heading over there now." He tucked his knuckle under her chin. "You'll be all right. And don't even think about signing any adoption papers. That boy needs his mother."

CALLEY SAT DOWN ON the cot and watched Riley walked out the steel-barred door. Her heart still raced. She reached up and touched her lips. Boy, he really knew how to get his point across. She still felt the bristle of his whiskers on her chin. The guard at the glass wall grinned. Her cheeks warmed. She reclined on the cot and rolled onto her side. Riley's arms around her made her feel grounded, safe, and secure. Could it be he really cared for her? Could this be a lifetime and not a moment thing? Her body relaxed for the first time in days, and her eyes closed.

A noise rattled her. She woke, not sure how long she'd been sleeping. Ty Davenport, from the wedding, followed another man into the detention area. The stranger had harsh features. His shoulders were rigid, his eyes angry, and his lips tight. He was speaking to Silvi. "You have two choices. Either set us up in an interrogation room or open the door."

Silvi walked behind them, glancing at the deputy behind the glass wall. These men clearly had her flustered. "The sheriff will be back any minute."

Ty glanced over at Calley, then turned to Silvi. "Howard tends to get carried away. He's usually more polite than this."

Howard turned on Ty. "We are here to interrogate a suspect, not play nursemaid to some officer's girlfriend."

Ty raised one of his eyebrows. He wasn't very tall, but what he didn't have in height, he made up for in muscular stature. His t-shirt was tight across his chest and biceps. Calley figured he could knock this Howard guy through a wall with just two fingers.

Calley leaned up on one elbow. "I really don't know who this guy is, but I don't think I like him very much."

Howard narrowed his eyes. "I really don't care if you like me or not."

Calley rose and walked over to the bars. "I'll tell you what. Why don't you let Ty interrogate me, and you go wait in the car?"

"You have no say in the matter."

"Very well. You can talk to my lawyer instead." She returned to the cot and pulled her feet up off the floor. She didn't like the way this guy treated Silvi, and Calley imagined he hadn't been any nicer toward the rest of Riley's staff. "Now, if you don't mind, I'd like to get some rest."

Howard's jaw tightened. He turned to Silvi then Ty. His breathing intensified when he got no help from either.

He glared at Ty. "Take her into a room. Find out everything she knows. I'll be waiting for the sheriff."

Calley didn't move until Howard walked out the door.

"What's going on?" She knew from meeting him at the wedding, Ty was with the DEA. Could that mean even more trouble for her?

"Come on." The door clicked and slid open. "Let's go somewhere more comfortable."

She followed him into a room like the one she'd met BJ and Allison in earlier. He held a seat for her to take.

"How are you holding up?" His voice was gentle. Calley hoped he wasn't trying to bait her by being nice.

"Wonderful." She looked over at the stocky man. She imagined he made a good agent with his muscular frame and dark looks. "How about you and Rayleene?"

"We're okay."

"Having problems?" From the look on his face, he didn't want to talk about it. "Hey, someone else's problems might make me feel better about mine."

"Let's just say it's hard to work on a marriage when you're not around."

"I'm sorry. So what is it you need? Didn't bring me a cake with a file, did ya?"

"No." His featured softened when he grinned. "What do you know about Peter Jameson's legal practice?"

"His legal practice? Why?"

"I wish I could tell you, but I can't."

"Honestly, I don't know much. He said he was a partner in a firm, and they handled all types of rich business clients. I never really asked him much about it."

"He never told you who any of these rich clients were?"

"No." What had she gotten herself into?

"Where did he take you when you went out?"

"We went to restaurants, mostly on the beach. My place." She really didn't want to talk about this. What if she was digging herself into another mess that she couldn't get out of? "I'm not going to say anything else until you tell me what's going on."

He glanced at the mirror on the wall. It was seconds before Calley realized Howard was probably listening in. Ty didn't speak, just sat there. His cell phone vibrated. He leaned back in the chair and read the text message. He nodded.

"It seems evidence in a drug sting has gone missing. And Peter Jameson was the attorney representing the accused."

Calley tried to draw everything in. She really didn't know much about Peter. She was always in such a hurry to find someone who would love her that she never asked any questions.

RILEY HATED THE IDEA of leaving Calley locked up, but the sooner he found out who was doing this, the safer she'd be. He and Deputy Green sat down the road in the police cruiser from the rental home Fifi Jameson was staying. Riley looked at the wedding photograph.

"Right here." A large grin sat on Deputy Green's face.

Green pointed to a picture of the wedding cake being cut. In the far corner, hiding behind everyone, was Fifi Jameson.

"I'll be." Riley grinned. This could be the break they were looking for.

"Do you think this will help, Calley?"

"We'll have to wait to see. But it's certainly not going to hurt."

"I hope so. I hate BJ being mad at me."

"Me too. Come on."

Green pulled the cruiser up the road and parked in front of the small home. The house lay just inside the city limits. Riley was grateful for that. A couple more feet, and he'd lose any chance of being the one to question her.

The home was more of a cabin, like the ones that bordered the lake. This one lay back in the woods, surrounded by trees. Riley stood outside the car, checking the area. A pier in the back floated in the lake. Convenient if you wanted to dump a body. He didn't see any boat she might have used to transport her dead husband out to the middle of the lake. But that didn't mean she didn't have access to one.

Riley had just stepped onto the porch when his cell phone rang. It was Silvi.

"Sheriff," she whispered. "I just wanted to let you know the DEA is here questioning Calley."

"The DEA? You shouldn't have allowed them." He crumpled the edge of the file in his hand. What had Calley gotten herself into now?

"One was pretty forceful. He just kind of came in and took over. The other is that friend of Matthew's."

Riley stood for a moment. He needed to get back to protect Calley, but that would give Ms. Jameson more opportunity to disappear if she were the guilty party.

"Get someone in there to listen in on what's being said. And if she sounds like she's about to say something she shouldn't, stop her." Riley relayed the information to Green. "Let's get this over with so I can head back."

Mrs. Jameson answered on his first knock.

She led them into a large living room with a white stone fireplace and oversize furniture. A large flat-panel television, Riley guessed to be about fifty inches, hung over the fireplace.

"I understand you're holding someone. A woman."

Riley decided to play along. "Yes, a Calley Regan. Do you know her?"

"No. Was she someone my husband represented?" Fifi leaned her head against her hand as she sat on the large tan sofa.

"No." Riley wasn't impressed with how easily she lied. "She wasn't a client. In fact, she was having an affair with your husband."

Fifi gasped. "I don't believe it."

"Really? You accosted her in the local grocery story over the affair. If need be, we can get the store's video to prove it."

Pink creased Fifi's cheeks, and she cast her eyes downward. "I did. It wasn't one of my better moments."

"So, you knew about your husband's affair?"

"Affairs. There were many." She nodded. "I just couldn't seem to leave. There was something about him that kept me connected."

"How long have you been in town?"

"Since I followed Ms. Regan. I shocked her pretty hard." Fifi gave a weak smile. "Most of the girls tell me how he's going to leave me. Ms. Regan looked like a bunny trying to scurry from a wolf."

From the glint in Ms. Jameson's eyes, Riley figured she enjoyed humiliating Calley in the middle of the supermarket.

"Then she called my husband to let him know what I did. He wasn't thrilled since she left a message with his legal assistant. By the end of the day, the other partners had called him in about it. I guess they were worried she was a client."

Good for Calley. Riley forced himself not to say it out loud. "Where were you this past Saturday, between two and six?"

"Here. I don't think I left once."

"Not once?"

"No." Red lipstick clung to one of her front teeth.

Riley pulled out the wedding photograph and tossed it on the table between them. "Then how did you end up at a wedding you weren't invited to?"

Tears welled in Fifi's eyes. She lowered her head into her hands and sobbed. Riley couldn't be sure how much was an act. He didn't move.

"Peter showed up here and told me his affair with that girl was none of my business. He said if he could get her back, he'd find a way. My guess is she wanted nothing to do with him after she found out he was married. But for him, I could tell she was different." Anger overtook her sorrow. "He'd fallen in love with this one. Saturday morning, I followed her. I wanted to catch them in the act. Have enough evidence to either force him to come back to me or pay highly for any divorce he wanted."

"But he never showed up at the wedding."

"I don't know where he went. And I could tell she wasn't pining away for him either." She grinned at Riley. "By the way, congratulations. You two make a wonderful couple. When's the baby due?"

"Month and a half." Riley couldn't get a read on this woman. Her emotions were too off kilter to get a handle on her.

"I see she didn't waste any time waiting on Peter. Good for her."

"Ms. Regan's gun was used to kill your husband. It went missing at the wedding."

"And you saw I was there, so you naturally assumed I did it." She shook her head. "How would I have gotten hold of her gun, Sheriff?"

"She dropped her purse, and everything fell out."

"I wouldn't know. I left after you two got up and started dancing. It was pretty obvious she wasn't waiting for Peter to show up." She rose and walked to the fireplace. "This may sound strange, coming from me, but I'm not even sure she had a reason to kill him herself."

Riley tried to hide his shock. Why would this woman be protecting Calley? Please don't let her have another secret. "What do you mean?"

"It was obvious from the way she looked at you. The way she clung to you while you danced. And the way you held her." Sadness floated into Fifi's eyes. "Peter and I used to look at each other that way. Besides, I'd followed Calley a couple of months ago, to and from work. She just didn't seem the type to kill a man over a breakup."

"What type does she seem?" Riley hoped no one noticed his face warm up from Ms. Jameson's words.

"Independent." She laughed, and tears flowed from her eyes. "Unlike me. I'm not sure how I'll survive without Peter."

"Did you and your husband have any children?"

"No. Peter never wanted them. I always hoped he'd change his mind, but he didn't."

"Maybe he did this time? Calley Regan is pregnant with *his* son."

Fifi gasped. "Peter's son?" She picked up her husband's photograph from the mantle. "You're wrong, Sheriff. I didn't kill my husband because of some pregnant woman. And if Ms. Regan did do it, it was because he wanted nothing to do with the child."

RILEY PACED. HOW DARE the federal government send their men down to manhandle someone on his turf. He had yet to unclench his fists. Calley seemed reasonably calm through the ordeal.

"We just need to know if Jameson ever met with any of these people." Howard said. He tossed six mug shots down in front of where Calley sat next to Riley.

"Who are they?" Riley fingered through the pictures.

"Known drug dealers."

Calley reached over to pick up the pictures, but Riley placed his hands on top of hers. "Before Ms. Regan gives any type of ID, we want an exchange of information."

"What type of information?" Howard's brow creased.

"I want to know where Eddy Fulbright is. He's an informant for one of your men, and he's disappeared."

"How are we supposed to know who's even protecting him?" Howard's face reddened. "We don't keep that stuff on computer."

"Without it, no further questions." Riley didn't want to get cocky with his attitude now that he had something to trade. "I have reason to believe he's responsible for a murder here in Lincolnville."

"Well, we don't know anything," Howard sputtered. "We can't give you something we don't have."

Riley pushed the photos back in front of Howard. "I suggest you find out if you ever want Ms. Regan to look at these pictures."

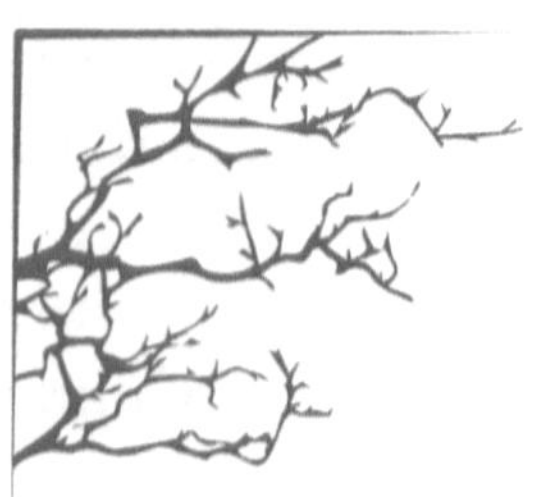

17

Riley reclined in his chair and dozed for a while. When Calley fell asleep the night before on his office sofa, he didn't have the heart to wake her and send her back to a cell. He recalled her laughter when he'd asked BJ to bring them supper the night before. She prepared Salisbury steak for Calley and a peanut butter and jelly sandwich for him. He was grateful Calley shared some of her dinner.

How could a woman be so beautiful with her hair a mess and no make-up? Every once in a while, she'd moan and shift positions.

They had yet to hear back from Ty or Howard about the whereabouts of Eddy Fulbright. Riley wasn't sure Calley would be of any help with the case the DEA was working on, but at least it gave them something to bargain with.

He motioned Silvi in before she had a chance to knock.

"It's the Prosecuting Attorney's Office. Line two," she whispered.

Riley nodded and picked up the phone. "Riley Owens."

"Sheriff, it's Ken Knight."

"How can I help you?"

"I understand you're holding Calley Regan for the murder of the vic found in the lake the other day?"

"She's more in protective custody." He grinned as he spoke the words.

"From what?"

"She was attacked in Atlanta before coming down here. The deceased was a guy she was dating. I think it's a high coincidence."

"I agree. Any suspects?"

"No."

154

Silence crawled over the line. It was seconds before Knight spoke again. "I heard a bullet from a gun she owns matched the murder weapon."

"It did. But the gun was stolen."

"Never reported. At least not to my knowledge."

"No sir. She wasn't aware of it." Riley sat forward, his elbows on his desk. "Her purse was dumped over at a wedding this past weekend. Plenty of people had the opportunity to pick it up. Including the widow and an uncle she'd testified against in a rape trial."

"It's no secret the relationship you have with this woman. Quite frankly, I don't want to hear about it. But we're getting a lot of calls about that girl. Some don't understand why she isn't sitting in the women's jail in Ringgold. Others don't like the thought of a pregnant woman in jail at all."

"She's not in Ringgold because she's not under arrest. And she's officially not in jail."

"Knock it off, Owens. We both know you've got feelings for this woman, so you're playing fast and loose with the law. I won't have any sense of impropriety on this case if I have to charge her down the line."

Riley washed his hand down his face.

"Either send her to Ringgold or let her go home." The man didn't say another word before he hung up.

Riley didn't like the thought of Calley sitting in a cell in Ringgold with a bunch of criminals. She deserved better. Besides, he knew deep in his heart someone was setting her up. He rose and walked over to the window. There was no way he'd send her over there. Lincolnville was his jurisdiction, and as such, he'd send her home and assign officers to protect her. That would be a much better choice than sending her to a jail miles away from him.

CALLEY WAS GLAD TO be back at the house with BJ. Even though she knew Riley was only trying to protect her, the idea of being in jail gave her the willies. Whereas, at the house, BJ spoiled her and looked after her. And the larger she got, the harder it was to do things for herself, like tie her own shoes. It also felt good to have Riley near her. She glanced over at him and smiled as she recalled their kiss at the jail.

"Are you sure you've had enough to eat?" BJ stood near the door on the front porch.

"I'm sure. You're going to keep going until I'm as wide as I am tall."

BJ took the pie plates and walked inside the house. Riley and Calley remained seated on the outside porch swing.

"You should know by now, no one goes hungry on BJ's watch." Riley had his arm around Calley on the back of the swing.

"I know. It wouldn't be so bad for me if the food wasn't so good. I just want to eat as much as I can stuff into my face. Which these days is quite a bit."

"I guess I need to be heading back to work. You need to get inside."

She longed to sit in the sun all day, but Riley gave strict orders she wasn't to go outside without him. "Umph." The baby kicked inside her belly. She placed her hand on her stomach as the baby moved. "I think he enjoyed that meal, also."

"I read somewhere that they get more active because they're turning into position to come out."

"Must be getting close." She laughed. "He's going to town in there."

Calley took Riley's hand and placed it against her stomach. The baby gave him a good nudge.

"That's amazing," he said with a large grin.

He kept his hand in place for a few seconds, then moved it to her face. Their lips met and heat seeped into her. She knew it had nothing to do with the weather.

He leaned his head against hers and drew in a loud breath. "I don't know how you did it, Calley Regan. But you got hold of me good."

"It was my ploy when I first threw up on you."

Riley laughed out loud. "Like I said, I need to go to work, and you need to get inside." He stood and held his hand out for her to take so he could help her from the swing. "I'll see you at dinner."

"I look forward to it."

He kissed her on the cheek and guided her through the front door. As tough as it was sitting in the house all day, she could handle it knowing Riley would return later. The thought of his arms around her made her warm inside.

"You've got hold of me, too, Riley Owens." She waved as he drove down the drive.

THE DAY DRAGGED ON as Calley anticipated seeing Riley again. It felt good to know he seemed as interested in her as she was in him.

"Girl, you haven't taken that smile off your face all day." BJ made gravy for the stew while Calley peeled carrots in the sink. "Does it have anything to do with that kiss I saw earlier?"

Calley's face warmed. "What kiss?" She couldn't help but grin.

"What kiss? You mean there's been more than one?"

"I really like him, you know."

"He cares very much for you."

"I hope so. I'm just afraid once he thinks about all this," she swept her hand around her belly, "he'll realize what a mistake he might be making."

BJ put down the whisk. "What is it you believe he needs to think about?"

"He's getting a lot of baggage with me. If he wants a lifetime, he needs to realize I'm an instant family."

"That boy knows you've got a child coming. I think at times he's as excited as I am, though he doesn't show it." BJ placed an arm around Calley's shoulder. "Are you telling me you'd like a lifetime with Riley?"

Calley stopped peeling. She hadn't really thought that hard about their relationship. It just felt right having his arm around her and being with him in this house. "I'm not sure. I've never had much luck with men. Maybe it's more wanting someone to care for me. I didn't feel like I was loved much as a kid. Always in Allison's shadow and such."

"Well, you're definitely loved here." BJ gave her a squeeze. "But I want you to ask yourself a question. You don't have to answer out loud. But if Riley were to walk off tomorrow, just walk right on out of your life, how would you feel?"

Calley thought about the question for a good minute. Only one word came to her mind. "Devastated," she whispered.

BJ returned to Calley's side from the stove. "Sounds like love to me." She kissed the side of Calley's head.

Calley's eyes misted over. Yes, she did love Riley.

They stood that way for what seemed like minutes until a car door slammed out front. Calley's stomach jumped with excitement. Riley. It was only a little after three. He was early.

"Oh, phooey." BJ said, turning and looking out the window. "It's that old coot, James Newman, III."

"ANY WORD FROM TY DAVENPORT?" Riley asked Silvi after he returned from a call.

"Nothing. But you have a visitor." She used her head to point at Marylou Tyson.

Riley was in too good of a mood to groan. "Marylou, what can I do for you?"

"I thought I'd stop by and see how you were holding up."

Riley directed her to his office. "I'm doing just fine. What made you think I wouldn't be?"

He kept the door open, though he noticed her perfume wasn't as harsh as usual. She took a chair in front of his desk. He sat on the opposite side.

"I heard about Calley getting arrested. I knew you were kind of sweet on her. It must be hard to have to put someone in jail you care for." Marylou shook her head. "I can't believe she killed that man. It just goes to show, you never really know someone."

"She's no longer in jail." Riley hoped his face didn't show the smugness he felt. "In fact, we have two other suspects in line ahead of her for the murder."

"Oh? Well, good." Marylou's voice betrayed her true feelings.

Riley had never done anything to make Marylou think he thought of her as anything other than a friend. Yet, her being hurt by his actions, real or imagined, caused guilt within him. He never intended to hurt her or anyone else. He would have to find a way to put it right. Calley, being a woman, might have a suggestion.

"Let me ask you something," he said. "During the wedding, when Calley almost passed out, did you see anyone gather anything that had dropped from her purse?"

"No. Why?"

"Apparently she had a gun in her purse, and after the wedding, it was gone."

"Are you sure?"

"What do you mean?"

"Riley, it's obvious you've got feelings for this woman. I'd just hate to see you get hurt. What if she just said she lost the gun, but she really had it all along?"

CALLEY STOOD BEHIND BJ as she greeted James Newman. BJ had refused to allow him entrance into the house. His straight shoulders and head held high reeked of arrogance. It was a wonder he didn't drown in a rainstorm with his nose that far up in the air.

"I'm not trying to push you into anything. I just want you to consider what I can do for a child."

"What do you think you can give a child that Calley can't?" BJ had yet to unclench her jaw.

"I've got money to send him to the best schools in the area. There's a wonderful Christian school in Chattanooga. Being retired, I can give him all the time in the world. Take him fishing, out to ballgames. Give him good quality time."

"A lot of boys turn out good, even in working families," Calley said.

"I understand that. But right now, you don't have a husband. You only have friends who are willing to help. How long do you think it'll last until they get tired of taking care of someone else's baby? And with this murder hanging over your head." He shrugged and held his hands palms up.

"You arrogant ..." BJ took a step toward him. "Get off my porch. This is no longer up for discussion."

James turned, walked to the first step, then hesitated. He looked back at Calley. "I don't want to push you into anything you don't want to do. But you should consider the fact that no matter what, boys raised by single mothers have a hard time becoming men. And right now, you don't even have a job."

Calley swallowed hard. She knew he was right. It often took a strong woman with a firm hand to keep a boy from going bad. Did she have that type of strength?

"Now don't you worry about what that man had to say. You'll make a wonderful mother."

"Are you sure?"

"I'm positive. What a child needs more than a two-parent home is a lot of love. This one will be covered with it."

"I know. Thank you for protecting me from that *vile man*." Calley growled the last part. It was nice to have someone so caring in her life. "But he is right about one thing. I don't have a job." She straightened when she hit on an idea. Maybe Sheryl could help her with that.

RILEY HEARD THE GUITAR before he opened the door. BJ was in the kitchen fixing dinner.

He walked up and gave her a one-armed hug. "How's my favorite aunt?"

"What did you do? The only time you've ever been this affectionate is when you want something." BJ pushed back away from him.

"It's just my way of saying thanks for taking me in all those years ago."

"Right. You're home early. Dinner won't be ready for another hour."

"Things were quiet."

"They've been quiet before. That never sent you home this soon. I have a feeling it's got something to do with that girl in the other room."

"Maybe." He didn't bother to hide his good mood.

"If I didn't know any better, I'd say you were in love." Her eyes shined. "I'm so happy."

"Sounds like Calley's in the back."

"Yeah. We got us a visit from James Newman, *the third*." BJ spoke in a haughty tone. "Mr. High-and-Mighty. I wish God would shock him with a lightning bolt to show him he's not the great Christian man he thinks he is."

Riley's mood shifted from one of happiness to anger. "Is Calley all right?"

"Oh, she's fine. I just think people like that get her to thinking she's not good enough."

Riley walked back to Calley's room. She had the guitar on one side as she played. He stood in the doorway and watched her.

"Welcome home, Sheriff," she said. "As you can see, I've gotten too big to hold the guitar on my lap."

His good mood returned upon seeing the sparkle in her eyes. He walked in and sat on the edge of her bed. "I understand you had a visit today from Old-Stick-in-the-Mud?"

"No. That's you. According to BJ, he's Mr. High and Mighty."

"I guess I deserve that. I'm trying to change my nickname." He pushed her hair to the side. "Are you all right?"

"I'm doing good. Just wondering what type of mother I'll be. If I recall, someone once called me a flake." She raised her eyebrows at him.

Riley leaned over and kissed her on the cheek. "I think you'll be a wonderful mother. One who will not only care deeply for her children but show them what it takes to have fun."

"Thank you."

"How about going for a ride?"

"Okay." She scooted off the bed.

"Let me change first, then we'll head out." He walked to his room and removed his holster and tie. Excitement reared at being on the bike. It had taken years to repair, and now it was a job come to full fruition. He led Calley to the garage.

"You mean on the motorcycle?

"It's too beautiful of an evening to waste inside a car."

"Do you think it's safe? For the baby, I mean."

"I don't see why not. Just get the best grip you can and hold on tight. If you get worried, let me know."

Riley handed Calley a helmet and pulled the Yamaha out of the garage. She climbed on behind him after he started it. Her hold was natural. She must have ridden before. Her belly felt like a basketball in the middle of them. Heat engulfed him when he imagined how nice it would be to have her hold on once they no longer have the baby between them.

He drove for a little over twenty minutes before he killed the engine in a clearing. The view was amazing with the water as the lake swallowed the orange sun. He had his arm around Calley's waist. The last time she'd seen the lake, it had been something menacing, something ugly as it released Peter's body.

"I wanted you to have a different view of the lake than the one you had the other day."

"It's lovely." She looked up at him. "Thank you for letting me be the first person you gave a ride to."

"You're the only one I want behind me." He lowered his lips to hers. It didn't take much for him to know BJ was right. As hard as he'd fought it, he'd fallen in love.

18

It was a beautiful Wednesday morning to be out and about. Calley had been tired of being stuck indoors with such nice weather. BJ drove while Calley sat in the front passenger seat. Sheryl finished a chocolate milkshake in the backseat behind BJ, a fully loaded gun rack attached to the SUV window. They'd stopped at several small boutiques in Chattanooga and the surrounding small towns that sold baby clothes while they were out looking at empty shops that Sheryl had located. Now they headed back to Lincolnville. Riley had given them permission to leave the house as long as an officer followed.

Her memory of riding behind Riley on the motorbike the night before infiltrated her system. The aroma of his citrus wood cologne stayed in the forefront of her mind. She only wished she could have held him tighter. She recalled the warmth that rushed through her upon him, telling her she'll be a good mother. It meant a lot to her.

BJ pulled the car in front of a green store in need of a paint job. Maybe a different color would make it look more inviting. The glass windows reflected the sun. She hoped it didn't shine in causing the place to be hot. This was the third building they were going to look at. The one in Chattanooga was nice with the mural painting of children playing on one wall. However, Calley didn't care for the idea of having to cover it with artwork. BJ didn't like how far it was away from her home. The second, in Ringgold, was too small. This last shop was just outside the Lincolnville city limits.

"This one is just a regular store," Sheryl said. "But I think it might do well. It's closer to home and bigger than the last one."

The store was empty except for a few boxes. If Calley chose to purchase the building, she would have to replace the lighting with something brighter. There was a large front space. Plenty of room for art pieces. The windows were tinted nicely to keep the sun out. That would be good to keep paintings from fading.

"Good morning." An older woman using a cane walked out from the back. "Sheryl, nice to see you."

"This is Calley Regan, the one I told you about." Sheryl had her hands on Calley's shoulders.

"Oh my. You look about to burst, young lady," the woman said.

"I feel like it."

"Boy or girl?"

"Boy."

"Congratulations. I understand you're looking to open an art shop."

"Yes. I plan to take paintings and artwork on consignment, then once I sell them, give a portion of the money to the artist or owner of the piece. However, I need a large enough space to display them." She walked to the back. There was a kitchen area and three empty rooms. One of the larger rooms could be used for storage, another for meetings with potential clients.

"What type of business was in here before?" Calley studied the space, getting an idea of where items might go.

"It was a children's clothing store."

"Why are you closing up?" She glanced at the woman, hoping she didn't say there was an infestation problem or something similar.

"I've retired. My young ones are all grown up. The only reason I even opened it was so I'd be around for them." The woman walked into the middle room, which measured about ten by fifteen feet. "This was the room I watched my grandchildren in. It seems like yesterday they were underfoot."

Calley had never considered bringing the baby to work with her. The smaller room would be perfect for a bassinet. The more she wandered around, the more her vision grew. Art displayed in the outer room, a storage room, a meeting room, and a nursery. BJ could help if she liked. Calley's dream could become a reality. Her mind raced with ideas for her new store. She couldn't do anything until after the baby came. Maybe a grand opening in six months? She thought over the timing. It might work. Thankfully, she'd been saving for years. She had enough to pay the lease for two years, which would give her time to get the business up and running. The only bad part was that Eva wouldn't be there to share it with her. She would love to have made her new store an offshoot of Eva's, but the shop had closed within a month of her death.

She glanced over at BJ and Sheryl. They both nodded with smiles on their faces.

A grin came over Calley's lips. This could really work. She turned to the woman who stood at the front door. "I'll take it."

CALLEY STARED UP AT the cross. It was such an ominous feeling to be sitting in her grandfather's church. Would he have love in his heart for his wandering granddaughter? At least she didn't need to worry about God. She knew He forgave her.

She didn't turn at the sound of the door closing figuring it was BJ. Calley was thankful Phyllis, the church secretary, had told her she could come to the church to rest. The officer he had watching her stayed in the reception area to give her some privacy.

A subtle hint of perfume hit her. An unfamiliar woman walked up and stood next to the pew Calley sat in.

"It's a beautiful sanctuary. Isn't it?"

"Yes, it is." Calley felt pride at the fact her family was responsible for it.

"I don't believe we've met. I'm Melanie Newman. James Newman is my husband." She extended her hand to Calley.

Calley hesitated before accepting it. "Calley Regan." She didn't want to discuss giving up her child. Not now.

"Do you mind if I sit?"

Without saying a word, Calley scooted down and gave her room.

"I understand you and my husband had a conversation regarding that baby of yours." She shook her head. "At Lydia's wedding, of all places."

"His timing is a bit off." Calley kept her eyes directed to the cross. "He also stopped by the house."

"He's been very excited the past couple of weeks. I thought maybe he'd made some sort of political deal, and he'd be vying for a senate seat." She paused. "I would have liked that better."

Calley looked at Melanie. Lines surrounded her eyes, and age spots dotted her face.

"You're a lovely girl, Calley. But I have no intention of raising your child. James has a problem with going off on his own without consulting others. He expects me to abide by his wishes because he's the man of the house. There are just some things I can't "submit" to." She used her fingers to do quotes in the air.

Tension released from Calley's shoulders. "I'm not giving the baby up anyway."

Melanie nodded and patted Calley's leg. "One bit of advice. A child needs a good Christian home. One where everyone abides by the Word, not just when it's convenient or in front of fellow churchgoers."

"I agree." Calley wondered if she was speaking from experience.

"Good. Do you have a strong relationship with God?"

Calley let out a laugh. "Not yet, but I'm working on it. It's been a while since I've felt Him with me. But some days I think He's coming back."

"I'm happy to hear that. Just remember, He's never left you. You might think He's walked away, but it's us who have done the walking. He's followed quietly, waiting for us to turn around."

Calley's vision blurred at her words. "I like the thought of that. Thank you."

Melanie rose from the pew. "I'll leave you in God's hands. I just like to come in to feel some peace before heading home. My husband is a politician. That means a lot of hot air."

Both women laughed.

"How are you doing living with Riley and BJ?" she asked.

"It's good. BJ spoils me."

"You should take advantage. Once the child comes, you won't get much of a break." Melanie took a step out from the pew. "I understand you've been good for Riley Owens. Some say since you've come into his life, he's loosened up a bit."

"He needed it. He was wound so tight, I'm surprised he didn't burst a spring."

"Yes, he was. I'm glad he's found you."

"I am too," Calley said under her breath.

Once Melanie left, Calley returned her attention to the cross. Melanie was probably right. It was Calley who'd walked away from God. Peace came over her at the thought that God never left her, and He was actually walking behind her the whole time. *Thank you, God, for putting good people in my life who care for me. And thank you for following me.*

RILEY GLANCED AT THE items for boys on the web. Should he go for a Brave's uniform? After all, Calley lived in Atlanta. She might be a fan. Or even a Falcon's football jersey. He picked up the buzzing phone.

"Yes."

"Riley, it's Ken Knight on line two." Silvi gave a bit of a laugh. "Do you want me to tell him you're busy?"

Riley glanced over his shoulder. She stood just outside the office window. His cheeks burned as he snatched up the phone. "This is Riley Owens."

"Riley. I understand you've let Calley Regan go."

"We didn't have enough to hold her on. Without the gun, we can't be sure who had it last. Either Her, the widow, or someone else with a motive who was also at the wedding."

"Did you search their houses?"

Riley swallowed. He'd let the ball drop. If Fifi Jameson had that gun, she'd have been smart enough to have gotten rid of it by now.

"I'm assuming your silence gives me the answer."

"I didn't even consider it." He ran his hand through his hair. "I actually believed both women, and I was there when Calley's purse got dumped over."

"I think you've let this woman get the best of you. That gun could be hidden right under your nose. I'm calling in a couple Ringgold detectives to search both locations."

"That's not necessary. I'll take care of it."

"You should have taken yourself off this case the moment your girlfriend was involved. No, Ringgold will handle the searches and the remainder of this case. I won't be able to get a search warrant until tomorrow."

"You don't need one for my house. I'll give permission."

"You can't for Calley Regan's room. A warrant will ensure there's no problem if we find anything. And Owens, you'd better hope we don't come across that weapon. It could mean your job."

Riley fumed. How dare Knight threaten him. Calley was more important than any job. He needed to get hold of Eddy Fulbright to get some answers. His prints were at Calley's home in Atlanta, and he was probably near Lincolnville at the time of Jameson's murder. Riley jerked up the telephone and dialed Ty Davenport's number.

"I still don't have anything," Ty said, not even waiting for Riley to say hello. "I'm still working on it."

"How important is this guy that the FBI would protect a killer?"

"Word is he's pretty high in a drug organization. A deal's supposed to go down, and he's going to lead us to the guys bringing a large shipment of heroin into the country."

"He's got to know his prints would show up at Calley's place." Riley ran his hand through his hair. "Can he be trusted?"

"That's the problem. Some are saying no." Ty let out a loud breath. "The people in the know are being very tight-lipped. I've got a call into a friend who works that department. He owes me, but I'm not guaranteeing he'll give up information about what's going on."

"I appreciate all you're doing."

"No problem. I like Calley. I can't see her being a killer."

Riley stared out of his office window. He agreed. He couldn't see Calley as a killer, either. The problem was his gut said Fifi Jameson wasn't one either. Of course, if he had to pick one, he knew it would be the widow who probably stood to inherit a lot of money. She had an even better motive. Her husband got another woman pregnant. Just because Peter Jameson claimed not to want children doesn't mean he didn't reconsider if her was in love with Calley. Sometimes people don't think they want a child until they're having one.

Riley's stomach growled. He'd worry about it after lunch. He walked out of the office. "Silvi, I'm heading home for lunch."

"You never used to go home." Silvi grinned. "By the way, I'd go with the Braves' uniform."

CALLEY HAD BEEN SO excited she must have talked Sheryl and BJ's ear off. They were probably thankful she asked to be taken to the church to rest while they continued shopping. After dropping Sheryl off at her house, BJ took Calley home so she could rest. She never used to get so tired shopping.

"I've done plumb wore you out. Haven't I?" BJ said as she drove them home. "I got a bit carried away with those clothes."

"You didn't hear me complain, did you?" Calley pulled out the white outfit BJ insisted on paying for. It was perfect for a baptism. All this shopping made her realize the time was getting near for the baby to be born. She only had a couple of weeks left, and she still needed to come up with a name. Maybe in a day or two she and BJ could sit down and go over some picks.

BJ drove the car up into the driveway. "If you can get those bags, I'll grab the rest from the trunk."

"I can take more than two."

"Oh, you got all that extra baggage already." She patted Calley's arm. "You go on inside."

Calley enjoyed how BJ mothered her. Once the baby came, and she was back to work, she'd have to find a way to thank her for all her kindness. Calley stuck the key in the lock and turned to see if BJ needed any help. She jolted when the door wrenched open.

She let out a scream. Eddy Fulbright, the man who killed Eva, grabbed her by the collar. He dragged her inside and threw her to the floor.

"You're early," he sneered.

"The police are looking for you. They know you killed my friend." Calley scooted herself into a corner.

"Don't matter. I'm protected." He grinned down at her.

"Please. The baby." Calley placed her hand on her belly.

"Don't need another brat in his world."

He held a gun in his hand. Her gun. She raised her leg up and kicked him in the shin. He let out a yell, and the gun went off. The bullet smashed into a picture on the wall above Calley.

"Stupid little…" He swiped a hand across his mouth. "I don't have time for this, any more than I got time to go after your friend outside."

He again turned the gun on Calley. This time, he was too far away for her to fight him. She rolled over and curled up in the corner, hoping he'd hit her and not the baby.

Calley jumped at the sound of the blast.

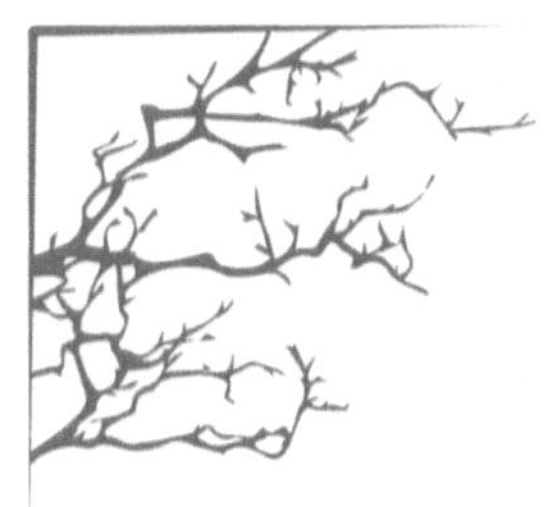

19

"Sheriff," Silvi said over the radio. "There's been a shooting at your house. There's already an officer at the scene."

Riley jerked the car around the corner and into the driveway. He'd have been earlier if it weren't for a guy speeding on Lomax Road. His mouth was dry as thoughts of dread rushed through him.

Deputy Hendrix was leaning against his car when Riley arrived home.

"What happened?"

"Let's just say you don't need me protecting your girl. Not with that aunt of yours around. Tom's inside with them. An ambulance is on the way."

Riley rushed through the open front door, his pulse pounding in his hears. BJ stood over a man, half his arm hanging by a few tendons, and blood covered the wall and floor. Tom, the other deputy, stood to one side, his focus on the man on the floor. Riley recognized the injured man as Eddy Fulbright. Calley was nowhere in sight.

"BJ."

His aunt turned to him, keeping the gun on Fulbright. "I guess this boy was in a hurry to meet his maker. I'm not sure I gave him much of a second chance."

"Crazy old lady." Eddy's words came out in short pants. "She tried to kill me."

"Don't worry, boy." BJ took a step back. "Ambulance is on the way. You might live, but that arm will never be useful again."

"I'll kill you for this, old woman."

173

"If I was you," BJ said, "I'd be getting things right with God, just in case." She bent down before Fulbright. "If you need someone to pray with you, I'd be more than happy to."

"Go to..."

BJ held up a finger. "Not me. And I could keep you from going there too."

Eddy rolled his eyes, then groaned out in pain.

Riley walked forward. He glanced around the room. "Where's Calley?"

"In your room. I put her in there with one of your guns until the police showed up. I thought it'd be safest until we could get the house secured."

Riley nodded. He dragged one of the dining room chairs over to Fulbright and cuffed him to it. A .38 lay on the dining room table in a plastic evidence bag.

"This yours." He lifted the bag over Fulbright's head.

He didn't speak. His face paled and sweat covered his forehead. Riley pulled back the man's shirt. The shotgun blast had torn off most of his arm. It was pretty bad. Only an act of God would save him now.

"Why are you after Calley Regan?" Riley said.

"Bite...me." Fulbright's breathing was harsh and deliberate.

"If you'd like, I'll ask him a few questions." BJ gave her nephew a wink. "You can just go wait down the road. I wouldn't want you to hear him scream."

As tempted as Riley was to allow his aunt to manhandle Fulbright to get answers, he knew he couldn't. It would go against every rule he believed in. He walked to his bedroom door and knocked.

"Calley, it's me."

"Come in." She was sitting up against his headboard. The gun beside her.

"Are you all right?"

"Yeah." She blew out a breath. "It's been a busy day."

RELIEF FLOWED THROUGH Calley as she sat in Riley's arms. With Eddy Fulbright arrested, she could actually breathe again.

"Your aunt really does know how to use a gun, doesn't she?"

"Yeah." Riley kissed Calley's forehead. "She was a marksman in the Army."

"I get the feeling there's a lot I don't know about her."

"I get the feeling I don't know all there is either." Sirens sounded up the road. Riley got up and looked out the bedroom window. "It's the ambulance and more officers. You can wait here. I'll take care of it."

Calley scooted off the bed. "I don't think so. I'm not letting you out of my sight until this guy is gone." She grabbed hold of Riley's arm and walked out of the room with him.

"What we got?" A paramedic walked in. He bent by Fulbright, felt his pulse, then turned to his partner. "He's lost a lot of blood. We need to get him in fast."

As much as Calley hated the man for killing Eva, she didn't want him to die. She turned her head away from the blood and grabbed hold of Riley.

They airlifted Fulbright to Chattanooga and the nearest trauma center. Technicians were still inside the house dusting for prints and asking questions. Calley had a hard time focusing on the answers. All she wanted to do was lie down. A couple officers straightened when a man in a dark suit and a red tie walked in. Even Riley's jaw tightened.

"Who's that?" Calley whispered to Riley, who sat beside her.

"His name's Ken Knight. He's a prosecuting attorney."

"Sheriff," Knight said with a raise of his head. "I understand you got Fulbright?"

"Yes sir. He's on his way to the trauma center in Chattanooga after he tried to kill Ms. Regan. My aunt stopped him." Riley wiped a hand under his chin. "By the way, he's the one who had her gun."

The man's eyes narrowed as he looked in Calley's direction. "How'd he get your gun?"

"I don't know," she said. "If I'd seen him at the wedding, I think I would have recognized him."

"You want us to believe this man, a stranger, walked into this house, carrying your gun? A gun used in the murder of your ex-boyfriend, and you don't know him."

"I don't. And I really don't care if you believe me or not."

"What reason could there be?" Knight stood with his feet spread apart and his arms straight at his sides.

"He tried to kill her with it. Speak with Ms. Jameson." Riley rose from the sofa. "According to the DEA, her husband was involved in drug activity. I can't help but wonder if he came across Mr. Fulbrite in his dealings or as an attorney."

"How did he get Ms. Regan's gun?"

"Ms. Jameson had sneaked into the wedding." Riley crossed his arms over his chest. "It's time you move on from Ms. Regan with all the other suspects who could be out there."

TWO DAYS PASSED, AND they were no closer to finding out how Fulbrite got Calley's gun. Riley tapped a pen on his desk between his two fingers. He turned his chair to face the window. It would be a nice day out on the bike. Maybe he'd take Calley for another ride this evening. He couldn't wait until the baby was born so he could feel her closer to him. Right now, her hands rested on his sides when they rode.

Once they no longer had that ball of a child between them, she could wrap her arms around him. A smile jerked at his lips.

He reached for the ringing telephone.

"It's Matthew Winters," Silvi said. "He's on line two."

Riley pressed the button. "Aren't you supposed to be on your honeymoon?"

Matthew laughed. "We're on our way back."

"How's Lydia?"

"Wonderful. She's shopping. She's also furious at you. Sheryl told her about you arresting Calley."

"Calling to warn me?"

"Yeah, bud." Matthew chuckled. "She wanted to leave the moment she found out, but Sheryl talked her out of it. Good thing BJ was there to fight for her."

"That she did. I thought I'd be eating peanut butter and jelly for a month." Riley stood and walked to the window. "Well, you tell Lydia not to worry. Calley's at the house, and I'm working to clear her name totally."

Silence came over the line. "Is there anything I can do?" Matthew said.

"No. I'm in touch with Ty. He's helping us out. You go enjoy that wife of yours."

"What about Calley?"

"What about her?"

"I've heard some rumors. You know how people talk." Matthew sighed. "I understand you two have gotten real close."

Riley swallowed hard. "Yeah, we have. Is there a problem with that?"

"I think it's great. Even Lydia approves. I just have one question."

"And that is?"

"Do you love her?"

A smile returned to Riley's face. He called it his Calley smile. Every time he thought of her, it crossed his lips. "Yeah, Matthew. I love her."

"And how does she feel about you?"

"I'm not sure." Riley hadn't really thought that far. He'd only realized his feelings in the last couple of days. "Either way, I can't help the way I feel."

"And no matter what happens, is it worth it?"

"Yeah."

He hung up from Matthew with a warm feeling in his heart. Something inside told him Calley felt the same. Whether she did or not, it was worth this feeling he had. Calley made him want to live life again. He would always owe her something for that.

The phone rang again. He hoped it wasn't Lydia ruining her honeymoon just to berate him.

"It's Ty Davenport," Silvi said. "Line one."

"Ty, apparently you didn't hear, but we found Eddy Fulbright." Riley couldn't help the smugness in his voice.

"I heard. The feds are pretty mad about him dying on the operating table. That's the bad news. The good news is they see no point in keeping his info a secret anymore."

Riley scoffed. "Yeah, now that the newspapers might get hold of the fact the government was protecting a killer."

"I just wanted to let you know they're sending the file over by e-mail. You'll be given the site and code to get to the information you need. I glanced at it and didn't see anything, but you're closer to the situation."

"I appreciate it." Riley gave his head a sharp nod once he hung up. Maybe now they'd get somewhere.

He rose and stuck his head out of the door and looked at Silvi. "Where's Green?"

"He went to grab some lunch."

Riley hadn't realized how late it was. "Call him and ask him to get me something, too. Then tell him I've got the Fulbright file coming in over the Internet. See if he can stay late tonight."

"Will do." Silvi slid off her chair. "And Sheriff... Riley, I'll stay as late as you need me to. We'll get this figured out." She gave him a reassuring nod.

"Thanks. I can use all the help I can get." Riley returned to his office. His vision blurred as he looked out the window. "Thank you, God," he whispered. "For putting such wonderful people in my life."

CALLEY LEANED BACK in the chair and patted her stomach. "Now that you're full, what do you want to do? I say take a nap. You've got BJ all excited. She's out shopping again. I have a feeling I'm going to have to be the mean guy, 'cause she's going to spoil you rotten. Of course, if Riley's any indication, she knows a bit about raising someone the right way."

She rose at the knock on the front door. That would be the third time the officer guarding her needed to use the facilities. You'd think he was the one who was pregnant. Riley had insisted she stay under protection until they got everything straightened out as to how Eddy Fulbright got her gun. Was it Peter's wife?

Calley pulled the curtain back and saw Marylou and Tiffany standing on the porch. Great, a bouncy baby and her two least favorite people in town. So much for a nap "Okay, God, I'll open up. But I'm leaving this in your hands. BJ's not here to protect me, so you have to."

She pulled opened the door. Two cars had parked in the driveway beside her own. "Hello, ladies. How can I help you?" The officer's cruiser sat back in the trees out of the sun. Even in the shade, he was probably hot. Calley thought about taking him a glass of iced tea once she got rid of her visitors.

"We've come to pick you up." Marylou rushed right in.

"Pick me up for what?"

"Now, if I tell you that, it wouldn't be a surprise." Marylou tugged at Calley's shirt. "You'll have to change. We can't have you looking sloppy."

A tomato soup stain trailed from Calley's chest to her stomach. "I make such a mess these days." She glanced between the two women. "Where is it we're going?"

"I said I couldn't tell you. Let's just say Sheryl asked me to come get you."

Euphoria set in. Sheryl had been hinting about a baby shower. Calley really liked that girl. "I like surprises. Let me change and use the bathroom. Come in and have a seat." She rushed back, put on a fresh shirt, and wrote a quick note, placing it on BJ's pillow. Of course, it was probably fruitless since BJ would be there.

Calley glanced around when she returned to the living room. "Where's Tiffany?"

"She's got a thing for police officers, so she's outside talking to your protector."

"Who doesn't?" Calley laughed. She pulled her purse around her shoulder and shoved her cell phone in her pocket before following Marylou to the car. Calley waved her fingers at Tiffany and the officer. Tiffany had a disappointed look on her face. She must have found out he was married. "Isn't Tiffany coming with us?"

"No, she needs to pick something up on the way so she's taking her own car. Also, she's letting the officer know where you're headed in case we lose him." Marylou then added, "I wasn't sure you'd want to come if it was only me. We haven't exactly hit it off since you got here."

"I'm sorry about that." Calley dropped into the front passenger seat of the Honda. A sharp pain hit her back. "Ooph."

"Are you all right?" Marylou fastened her seatbelt and started the car.

"Yeah. This kid just gave me a good wallop."

"It won't be long now."

Calley rubbed her belly. "I can't wait until I have him. I'm tired of being pregnant and want to see my feet again."

RILEY RUBBED THE BACK of his neck. There was a lot of information on Eddy Fulbright. Everything from his friends to his drug dealing comrades. Riley had split the file between himself and Green. Silvi had gone to pick her children up from school but was on her way back.

There didn't seem to be any connection between Fulbrite and Peter, or even Calley's uncle. Nothing in the police notes to indicate who might have been involved with Fulbrite.

"Anything?" He leaned back and stretched.

"No." Green who sat in a desk opposite.

"It doesn't make sense. There has to be something in here. Cally's not going to be safe until we find it." The cursor on the computer blinked at him as if mocking his lack of progress.

"Maybe he went after Calley by mistake."

"You don't go after someone twice over misidentification. No, he wanted her dead or in jail. But why?" Riley got up and paced the office. They must have missed something. "Switch information. Maybe we just missed it."

"How about I fix some more coffee?" Silvi walked in from the outer office.

"Sounds good." Riley nodded. "It's going to be a long night."

"I'll be back to help in a moment." She disappeared through the door to the conference room.

He scanned the friends of Eddy Fulbright. Maybe Riley needed to get information on each name in the file to see if they had a connection to anyone involved. There was a good chance Peter represented a friend of Fulbright's. Maybe Peter asked someone to take care of Calley for him. Fulbright could have been hired to do it. It's happened before where the person asked to do the killing hires someone else to do the deed.

Silvi placed the cup down in front of Riley. She picked up a photograph of a young Eddy Fulbright with two other men. Recognition filled her eyes.

"You know any of them?" Riley said.

"It's the tattoo I recall. Who is he?" She tapped her finger on the photograph.

"That's Eddy Fulbright."

"In his mug shot, he looks different, but I swear he's the same guy."

"Where had you seen him?"

"In a family photograph at a birthday party a couple of months ago." She flicked the photograph in her hand, her forehead creased as if trying to recall the circumstance.

"Whose?"

"Marylou Tyson's. I swear this is a guy in the picture I saw on her mantle."

"We need to talk to her." Riley rose from the table. Hopefully Marylou or someone in her family would know a connection between Eddy Fulbrite and one of the other suspects. He dialed BJ's number to give her an update.

"Hello," BJ answered.

"Anything new going on?"

"I'm just having tea with Tiffany. She was having a talk with your officer when I arrived. I think she likes him. Too bad he has a wife. I'm also upset that Sheryl didn't let me in on the surprise."

"What surprise?"

"I got a note from Calley saying she was meeting Sheryl for a surprise."

"Did she say where?"

"No. But Tiffany said she went off with Marylou."

A stone dropped into the pit of Riley's stomach. "Did the officer go with them?"

"No. He's still parked out front. I assumed you had someone following her while he watched the house." BJ paused. "Riley, what's going on?"

"I'm not sure, but keep Tiffany there, no matter what. I'm on my way." Something didn't feel right. Why would Sheryl have Marylou pick Calley up? And why would BJ not be in on it? She was closer to Calley than anyone in town.

Riley hung up his phone and tried Tom's number. No answer. If he was in the cruiser, he'd answer. Something was wrong.

Riley rushed from the conference room, yelling to Green. "Marylou's taken off with Calley, and Tom's not answering." He grabbed his car keys from his office. "Come on Green. Something's not right."

Once in the car, he put in a call to Sheryl.

"Hello, Sheriff. Does your girlfriend know you're calling me?" Sheryl's voice came across cheery.

"Is Calley there with you?"

"No. Why? Are you checking up on her?"

"I understand you have some sort of surprise waiting for her."

"Oh no. She found out about the shower. Lydia and I were trying to keep it quiet. We hadn't even invited anyone yet." She let out a harrumph. "How did you find out?"

"Marylou."

"What's Marylou got to do with anything?"

"She just picked Calley up and said you were waiting for her with a surprise."

"Riley, the shower isn't until next week after Lydia gets back." Sheryl's voice turned serious. "And the last person I'd have pick up Calley would be Marylou. Word is she hates Calley because you're in love with her."

20

Calley shifted in the car seat. That pain felt different. It wasn't really a kick. Sweat formed over her forehead. She leaned back and tried to get comfortable. The deserted road unnerved her. She didn't even see the officer following.

It was strange that Sheryl might have a baby shower before Lydia returned. Maybe she had a surprise for the art shop. Calley reminded herself to be patient. Pain shot through her back. She moaned.

"I think something's wrong." She turned to Marylou, who had her eyes on the road. It was darker than normal for the afternoon because of thunder clouds rolling in.

"What do you mean?" Marylou had what looked like a fake smile painted on her face.

"I don't know. It just feels different." Anxiety crawled into Calley. It was too early for the baby. She still had over a month before he was due.

"Don't worry. It'll soon be over." Marylou's features turned dark. Her eyes narrowed and her lips disappeared. "Riley's a good man." Her voice was low and tight.

"Yes, he is." Calley let out a loud breath. She panted like she'd seen women in labor do on television. Maybe she should have considered a Lamaze course. It was a bit late now to change her mind. The next jolt took her breath away. She grabbed Marylou by the arm, but she jerked free.

"Riley needs a good woman. Not some ready-made family." Marylou continued to stare straight ahead.

Calley had enough on her mind without dealing with some jealous woman who never even dated the man. "You need to turn around. I've got to get to the hospital."

"I don't think so." Marylou held one hand on the steering wheel. With the other, she grabbed hold of Calley's head and slammed it into the dashboard.

The blow stunned Calley. "What are you doing?" She grabbed her head. "Are you nuts?"

"Don't ever say that to me." She jerked Calley's head back by her hair. "My stepfather said that to me once, and I cut out his tongue." Marylou's bogus grin returned. "Just sit back and enjoy the ride. It'll be the last you ever take."

Anxiety grew in Calley. Her heart pounded and sweat rolled down from her forehead. Whether it was true what Marylou said about her stepfather or not, she was one seriously demented woman. Calley glanced out the window. The car was moving too fast for her to attempt a jump. The cell phone in her pocket vibrated.

"Don't even think about it," Marylou snarled. "You've caused me way too much trouble. All I heard after you left town was how much Riley liked you. It made me sick. It took months to get your address to take care of you. I guarantee I won't miss this time."

Calley swallowed hard. Pain again shot through her back again. Her hands ached from holding the grab-handle next to her head. *Please God, get me through this.*

NEITHER CALLEY NOR Marylou answered their phones. Tom was supposed to follow Calley no matter what. He still didn't respond. Riley had a nagging feeling in the pit of his stomach. He sped the car toward his home. Why would Marylou want to hurt Calley? Sheryl hinted she was jealous. Tiffany was the best bet for information. He screeched into the drive, spinning gravel up when he stopped. Deputy Green's hand jutted out onto the dash when the car jerked to a stop.

"Check on Hendrix." Riley nodded toward the car parked in the trees. Tiffany's sedan was still in the driveway.

He stormed into the kitchen. BJ held her shotgun in her lap. Riley gave his aunt a nod.

"You said to keep her here," BJ said. "She was insisting on leaving after our phone call. I made sure she didn't."

"She's gone crazy, pointing that gun at me," Tiffany said. "This is kidnapping."

Riley placed one hand on the table and bent down beside Tiffany. "Where's Marylou?"

"How should I know?"

"You said she was taking Calley to meet Sheryl."

"That's what Marylou said." Tiffany looked over at the gun in BJ's hands. "Your aunt said she was going to shoot me if I left. You need to get her some help. I didn't do anything wrong."

Green burst through the front door. "Hendrix is dead. Been a while. Looks like a puncture wound in the neck."

Riley wiped a hand across his mouth. He turned again to Tiffany. "I'm only going to ask you once. Where'd Marylou take Calley?"

"I don't know what you're talking about," Tiffany cried. "Marylou said she had a surprise for Calley."

BJ rose, the gun in her hand. "Except, when I pulled up, you were standing beside Hendrix's window. In fact, I thought you were talking to him. You had to know he was dead. Yet, you said nothing." She shook her head. "I should have called when he was still here. If anything happens..."

"This isn't your fault." Anger rushed through Riley. He jerked Tiffany up and backed her against the wall. "That's life for the killing of a cop. If you want any chance of ever getting out of jail, I suggest you tell me where Calley is." He braced his hands against the wall on either side of her head. "Now."

Tears flowed from Tiffany's eyes. "I told her not to do it. She was just so mad that Calley took you away from her. And then when I saw the dead officer, I knew she'd gone over the edge. I was scared."

Riley lessened his hold. "Where are they?"

"All she told me was that she was going to take her to Lincolnville Park. Strand her in the woods to prove she's not the right fit for you. She thinks you won't want Calley anymore if she freaks out and gets lost in the woods. She didn't say anything about killing anyone."

Riley released his hold. Tiffany fell onto her knees on the floor, her head in her hands as she sobbed. "She made me go along. She always made me go along."

"Get going," BJ said. "Vincent and I will take care of her."

"Green, take her in." Riley used his head to point at Tiffany. "Get as many as you can out to the park. Call the other counties if you have to."

Calley could be anywhere. Lincolnville Park was seven miles long and six miles wide. There was only one place to park unless you parked on the main road. Marylou probably wouldn't chance that. She'd use the parking area. Hopefully, someone would be there to help Calley if she needed it. But with the impending storm clouds looming, it was unlikely.

Riley pictured the parking area. Once you parked, you had to walk. The trails were too narrow for most vehicles. Looking for Calley on foot would take too much time.

"I didn't know she was going to kill her." Tiffany sniffled. "I didn't know."

Riley didn't care. That would be for the prosecuting attorneys to decide. He had to get to Calley. He pressed the button for the garage door and hopped on the motorcycle. Once started, he shot through the opening garage door.

CALLEY TOUCHED HER belly. She had to be in labor. There was no other explanation. "Do you know how to deliver a baby?"

"It's not going to come to that."

"Don't bet on it."

"Once we get to where we're going, you'll no longer feel any more *labor* pains." Marylou gave out a low laugh.

Calley's heart pounded. This can't be happening. Marylou had lost her mind.

Another pain hit Calley. She had to find a way to save the baby. "Even if I'm not here, Riley will raise it." She touched Marylou's arm. "He'll need a woman to help him."

Marylou jerked the car into Lincolnville National Park. "We'll have our own children. We certainly won't need yours." Marylou slammed on the brakes in the empty lot.

Calley flipped open her seatbelt and jumped from the car. She ran back to the street but didn't get far. Marylou caught up with her in just a couple of steps. She pulled Calley back by her hair.

"We're just going for a walk. It won't be long now." Marylou held a knife to the side of Calley's neck. "Just go in a mile or so, then I'll get you out of Riley's life for good."

"But everyone will know. Tiffany knows I'm with you. The officer."

"Tiffany won't say anything. She's more afraid of me than you are. And I already took care of your guard."

Calley's heart slammed against her ribcage. "I left a note for BJ."

"I don't believe you." She shoved Calley toward the path leading into the park. "Get moving."

"But wasn't it Eddy Fulbright who tried to kill me? I don't understand." Her feet scraped against the dirt trail.

"I paid my cousin to do you. He'd even be able to admit to it and get immunity from the government. Too bad he didn't turn out to be as good a killer as he was a talker."

Her cousin? Calley's memory flashed to a phone call she overheard Marylou take in the garage the day Riley got the bike to run. She paid the person on the phone to get the job done. Could Calley have been that job? If so, Marylou really was insane. Calley had always thought Tiffany was the meaner of the two.

She glanced around for any chance of escape. Hunters, hikers, anyone to help her. Pain shot through her sending her to her hands and knees. She sucked in a couple of deep breaths. A loud clap of thunder sounded overhead.

"No one's going to find you here until it's too late. Both you and that brat will be out of my life. Riley will then be all mine."

A large rock protruded from the ground next to Calley's right hand.

"Get up." Marylou used her foot to nudge Calley's side.

With every ounce of energy, Calley bound up and turned. Marylou had no time to react. Calley slammed the rock into the side of Marylou's head. She shoved Marylou off the path and raced toward the entrance of the park.

"You little... You won't get away." Marylou spoke in broken words.

Calley's ears rang. Dizziness rushed over her. She grabbed her chest and went down to the damp ground. She had to get to the road. The entrance wasn't even thirty feet away. The crunch of dried grass sounded behind her. Calley rolled over and kicked out at Marylou. The knife slashed her leg. Calley screamed. Marylou stood over her, slashing and stabbing. Calley put her hands up to protect herself. Her teeth clenched through the pain. Whether or not she made it, she had to protect her son. She jerked her leg out and caught Marylou off guard. She stumbled over. A motorcycle roared close by. There was no way she could get up and get his attention. She rolled over and crawled on all fours. Her head spun. She opened and closed her eyes to focus.

The motorcycle got closer.

"You shouldn't have taken him away from me," Marylou yelled.

The drone of the motorbike grew louder. Calley grabbed her stomach. Pain shot through her.

"It's too early," she cried. "It's too early."

RILEY NEARLY LOST CONTROL of the motorbike when he first saw Marylou standing over Calley with a knife in her hand. When he jumped at Marylou, his bike went down in a ditch. He twisted her onto her stomach and zip-tied her hands behind her back. Then he tied her legs so she couldn't run.

"But I did it for us," Marylou yelled. "I love you. And you love me. I know it." She quieted for a brief second. "Get these things off me," she screamed

He didn't care to listen to the words. He called Deputy Green on his cell. "Get an ambulance over here. And Green, hurry."

Calley let out a loud moan. Riley dropped to his knees beside her. She fought off his touch.

"It's me. It's Riley."

She stopped flailing her arms and blinked a few times before grabbing hold of his sleeve. Blood saturated her shirt. Her bloody hands and arms were covered in dirt. He brushed her hair from her face.

She grabbed hold of him by the collar. "The baby. It's too early." Tears fell from her eyes.

He reached down and touched her belly. Even though his heart pounded against his ribcage, Riley knew he had to keep calm for Calley's sake. "Nah. He's a strong kid."

Her lip trembled. She had yet to let go of him.

"You're both going to be fine." He bent over and kissed her forehead.

"Please," she gasped. Her eyes desperate with fear. "Promise me. If I don't make..."

"Shh. Save your strength. Nothing's going to hap—"

She placed her fingers over his lips. "Promise me." Her voice weakened.

"Anything." He bent closer to hear her better.

"You'll take care of my son. Our son." She placed her hand on the side of Riley's cheek.

"I promise." He kissed her hand. Her grip tightened, and she gasped.

Riley looked up when a car skidded to a halt. Green ran up. "An ambulance is about two minutes away," he said.

Riley glanced over his shoulder at Marylou. "Take her out of here."

Green cut the zip-tie around her legs and lifted Marylou from the ground. She screamed and kicked at him, but Green was strong enough to drag her back to the car.

Calley let out a yell. She breathed in spurts. Her eyelids fluttered and her eyes rolled back.

"Calley! Calley, don't close your eyes." Riley placed his hand on her cheek. "Calley!"

She opened her eyes. "When'd you get to be such a nag?"

He let loose a laugh. "When I fell in love with you."

"I love you, too."

Paramedics rushed up. Riley hadn't even heard their vehicle pull in. "What've we got?"

"She's been stabbed in the arms and legs. I think she's in labor." Riley kept hold of Calley's hand. "She also has high blood pressure and suffered a heart attack a couple of months ago." He knew he had to tell them as much as possible to give her every chance of survival.

One paramedic took notes while the other used a stethoscope to listen to Calley's heart and the baby. "We need to get her in. She's losing a lot of blood." He forced Riley aside.

Calley's body shivered, and her eyes fluttered again. Helplessness drifted over Riley as they lifted Calley onto a gurney. She let out another yell.

"You can ride up front." A paramedic smacked Riley on the shoulder.

Rain drops sprinkled down over them as they rushed to the ambulance. Riley was forced to sit in the front passenger seat, the siren sounding overhead. He listened and prayed, not knowing what was going on in the back of the vehicle. The paramedic in back constantly gave updates to the driver who sat on the radio with the local hospital.

"She's going into cardiac arrest," the paramedic in the back yelled.

Riley's grip tightened on the armrest.

21

Riley trudged into the hospital chapel. He stared up at the cross. His legs folded, and he dropped to the ground. "Please God, don't take either of them. I promise I'll be a good man to her." He sobbed. "Even if she doesn't want me, please don't let them die." His face fell into his hands as tears flowed.

A hand on his shoulder drew his attention. He looked up with blurry eyes at BJ, who stood over him. She got down on her knees and pulled him into a hug.

"There, there." Her voice was soft and comforting. "Calley's a lot stronger than even she realizes. But you let it out if you need to. You've been through a lot in your life. Too much." She kissed the top of his head.

Riley didn't know how long he stayed in BJ's arms before they moved to a seat. He brushed at his eyes. What if the baby made it and Calley didn't? He'd made her a promise. One he intended to keep. He only hoped he could live up to her expectations of him as a father.

"I told her." He choked. "I'd take care of the baby, if..." He couldn't finish. The thought was too horrific.

"*We'll* take care of him. Raise him the way Calley would want, with lots of love." She sniffled.

BJ took a tight hold of Riley's hand. He looked into her eyes. Concern covered her face.

"I need to call her mother, I suppose." Riley brushed at tears.

"I did. She said she didn't care, and it'd be best if the baby didn't make it." BJ shook her head. "How can a woman be so cold?"

194

Riley shook his head. "Calley and the baby have got to make it, if for nothing else, to make the old bat angry." Silence fell between them. "She's got to," he whispered.

"She will. She will."

"Excuse me," Sheryl Coufield stuck her head in the door. Tear streaks lined her face. "Riley, there's a nurse out here at the desk looking for you."

Somehow, Riley stood on his unstable legs, his aunt's arm around him. When he got to the door, he pulled Sheryl into a hug and kissed her on the cheek.

Tears fell down Sheryl's face. "She's going to be all right," she said. "I know she is."

Riley nodded. Matthew and Lydia, who sat in the waiting room across from the chapel, rose when he walked out. They both pulled him into a hug. It was good to have such good friends at a time like this.

He trudged to the nurses' station, expecting bad news. "I'm Riley Owens. I understand someone's looking for me." His voice quivered.

"We need your information and for you to sign this." The woman handed a form to Riley.

"Are Calley and the baby all right?"

"The mother's still in surgery. They had to perform a C-Section. He's a tiny thing but has a good set of lungs. They're checking him over." She patted Riley's arm. "I'll go back to see if I can get an update."

He stared at the document the nurse had given him. His heart leapt to his throat. It was an information form for the baby. The name Calley had given them for the boy was Riley Owens, Jr. She'd left the middle name blank. He grunted a laugh. She'd never asked him what it was. He filled in Michael. Tears blurred his vision as he glanced at the father's name. Riley Owens. He wrote in his address and the rest of the information requested. When he came to the signature line, he breathed in a deep breath and paused. The form wasn't a birth certificate, so he'd have to get a lawyer to see how to become the child's father legally.

"It's a big step." BJ placed her hand on his arm. "If you're not willing to go all the way with this, you need to stop now."

"I just hope she doesn't change her mind when she comes to her senses." The pen flew across the line. He touched Calley's wobbly signature.

"Mr. Owens. They'll be bringing Ms. Regan to Room 220 if you'd like to follow me."

Riley and the others didn't speak while they followed the nurse to the room. A small window looked over the parking lot. It was dark out.

Another nurse walked in, pushing a neonatal crib. She picked up a small object in a blue blanket. "Would you like to hold your son?"

Riley looked down at the tiny boy. "I don't, I don't know how."

"Hold him like a carton of eggs, not a basketball." BJ grinned through tears.

Riley sat in a chair in the corner, and the nurse placed the baby in his arms. He hardly weighed anything. "Are you sure he's all right? He seems so small."

"He's going to be just fine."

The baby squeaked when he yawned. His mouth was so tiny. How could any sound emanate? Riley hoped he wasn't holding him too tight.

"And Calley?" He looked up at the nurse.

"They'll be bringing her in soon."

"So, she's all right?"

"She's weak after everything she's been through. While a couple of stab wounds were deep, most were superficial. And the stress on her heart lessoned once she gave birth." She pointed to the baby. "I need to take him back now. Once his momma comes down, I'll bring him back."

Riley didn't want to give their son back. At that moment, it was the closest thing to Calley he had to hold on to. He glanced over at the four people staring down at him. They smiled. He rose and returned his son to the nurse. His son. *His son.* The words caused his heart to warm and happiness to soar inside.

"She's going to be all right." He laughed out loud. "Everything's going to be all right."

THE SLASHING. THE BABY. Marylou standing over her. Calley woke with jolt.

"It's all right," a familiar male voice said.

She glanced around. She was in a room. Riley stood beside the bed. Her mind worked to remember. The ambulance ride. The hospital. A bandage covered her left arm from her hand to her elbow.

She jerked upright. "The baby?"

"He's beautiful and healthy," Riley said. "You're going to be all right, too."

"Marylou?"

"She's at the Sheriff's station in Ringgold."

Calley remained silent while she scanned the room. She cried and laughed at the same time. "Wow. I had a baby."

"You sure did. Of course, you could have done it without all that excitement." He bent over and kissed her forehead.

"What can I say? I like a lot of attention." She glanced at the foot of the bed. "That's wonderful."

"What is?"

"For the first time in months, I can see my feet move."

Riley shook his head. His face turned serious. "I talked to the office. Marylou confessed to sending her cousin Eddy Fulbright after you.

Apparently, Peter Jameson caught her watching you when you returned to Lincolnville. He threatened to let everyone know she was stalking you."

"I never saw her."

"Apparently no one did. Jameson told her if she didn't find a way to get you back to Atlanta, he'd make her life miserable. I think he might have been in love even if you were pregnant, no matter what he'd said."

"I wouldn't have cared one way or the other."

"Good for you. Of course, you dropping your purse at the wedding gave Marylou the opportunity to kill Peter and set you up." He took hold of Calley's hand. "I'm sorry you had to go through all of this because of me."

"Yeah, you owe me big time." She gave him a smile.

"That I do."

"Imagine if you'd married her. One night you'd come home and tell her she overcooked the okra. That is not a pleasant thought." Calley's shoulders shuddered.

"No, it's not." He played with Calley's fingers on her right hand.

"I hope you don't mind. I listed you as the father in case anything happened." She paused. "I didn't do it to trap you. It doesn't have to go any further than that form. I just wanted to make sure my mom couldn't get custody."

"I don't think so. You're stuck with me. One thing I noticed was you didn't have my middle name down, yet you called him a junior."

"I didn't know it. It's not something weird like Wilbur, is it?"

"It's Gomer."

Calley gasped.

Riley laughed. "No, it's Michael."

"Not funny."

"Now, where's *your* sense of humor?" Riley sat on the edge of the bed. "BJ's downstairs buying the baby his first birthday present. She'll be up in a few minutes."

"She's going to spoil that kid."

"Yes, she is. I got his mother a present also. I picked it up first thing this morning. My big plan was to take you for a ride and give it to you while we watched the sunset. Unfortunately, the rain and other things ruined that idea." Riley pulled a small box out of his pocket. When he opened it, a gold solitaire sparkled in the light.

Calley didn't know what to say. It was beautiful.

"Calley Regan, will you do me the honor of spending the rest of your life with me?"

She nodded. She was speechless as he slid the ring over her finger. He bent over and gave her a warm, passionate kiss. A knock interrupted their moment.

"Come in," Calley said.

"Someone's here to see you." A nurse rolled in a see-through crib.

Calley adjusted in the bed so she could sit up further. The nurse held the baby in her arms, waiting for Calley to get situated. Her left arm hurt, and so did her stomach. Disappointment rushed in at the thought of not being able to feel her child in her arms.

"I want to hold him," she said. "But with my arm, I can't."

"I've got an idea." Riley shifted next to her on the bed. He tucked one arm behind Calley, and she leaned back against him. The nurse placed the baby in Riley's left arm, so the child was in front of Calley.

She touched her son's face. "He's so beautiful. Hello RJ." She leaned deeper into the crook of Riley's arm. "It's hard to believe something that small came out of that big ball."

Riley kissed her cheek. "You did a good job."

The nurse left them, and they held the baby until BJ and Sheryl came in. BJ had her arms full of balloons and a small blue teddy bear.

"What'd you do, buy out the store?" Calley said.

"Not quite. She missed a few items." Sheryl gave Calley a hug. "Lydia and Matthew had to head to the church for a meeting, but they're coming back up later this evening."

BJ passed the bear over to Calley and the baby. "Allison said she's planning to come up later today, also." She paused and picked up Calley's left hand. "Is that what I think it is?"

"Yes." Calley glanced over at Riley. "He's stuck with me now."

"Oh, wonderful." Sheryl clapped her hands. "I get to plan another wedding."

Riley's hold tightened on Calley. She could tell his breathing increased against the side of her head. Just what he'd want, something large and formal.

"A small one," Calley said. "Only close friends and family. I don't think a woman with a child should have a large ceremony. I've always thought that was a bit pretentious."

"Don't worry," Riley said. "I'm sure Sheryl can still work wonders, even on a small affair."

After several minutes of discussing wedding plans, BJ placed the gifts and cards out on display. Calley relinquished her hold on the baby so the others could hold him. She hadn't realized she'd fallen asleep until she woke up. The light from the hallway shined in on the chair next to her. Riley leaned forward, RJ in his hands.

Calley smiled as she listened to him talk with the baby, his voice low and gentle.

"I'll teach you how to fish and play ball. And once you get older, I'll tell you all about the best day of my life. It was when I first met your mother. You're not going to believe what she did to me."

The End

Check out the next in the Lincolnville
Mystery Series:

One Last Breath

One Last Breath

1

BJ OWENS RUSHED INTO the Catoosa County Sheriff's substation in Lincolnville, Georgia. She didn't bother to stop at the reception desk, instead marching straight back to the sheriff's office. She burst through the door.

"What have you got for me?" She stared down at her nephew, Riley Owens.

He held a manila folder out to her. "By the way, the family's fine."

"I have a few other things on my mind right now." She jerked the file away. "Besides, I just saw them yesterday. I know they're fine." She glared down at him.

"Do you think Lyndsey will listen?"

"I don't know." What BJ did know was she had to get her great-niece away from this creep she'd been dating. The thunderstorm shook the windows as if to shudder its own dislike of the man.

"Sit. I'll get you some coffee." Riley walked around the desk and filled a cup from the pot on a filing cabinet in the corner.

BJ sat down in the wood chair on one side of Riley's desk. He passed her the mug, and she took a sip of coffee. The rich hazelnut flavor did little to ease her mind. She rubbed her eyes, gritty from lack of sleep. After a moment, she opened the file folder.

At the age of nineteen, Cliff Mason was convicted of possession of a controlled substance – cocaine. Currently, twenty-six, the authorities suspected him of getting close to teenagers, both male and female. Mason was on a list of possible child traffickers in the south. He'd been with at least three of four children who had disappeared. But so far, the authorities didn't have enough evidence to arrest him, much less convict.

BJ's stomach jumped with each word she read in the report.

She next stared at his mug shot to memorize his face. With his boy-next-door good looks, it was no wonder these kids fell under his spell. So young to be on the road to hell. BJ's pulse raced as she stared into his emotionless brown eyes.

She shuffled through several pictures of missing children, eventually fixing her gaze upon a photograph of a sixteen-year-old girl who'd disappeared from her home in Miami more than two-and-a-half years ago. The police found Bernadette Lewis' strangled body in a culvert near Orlando almost a year after she went missing. Mason had been her boyfriend at the time she disappeared.

BJ stared at the headshot of Bernadette, a school logo in the upper left corner of the photo. The young girl had been a beautiful thing. Wavy blond hair and green eyes that caught your attention, especially against the dark blue backdrop. She could almost pass for a younger version of Lyndsey, Mason's current girlfriend.

BJ took another sip of coffee to moisten her dry throat.

Thunder blasted again overhead.

BJ stared at Bernadette's picture. "Mason's definitely got a type," she whispered. As long as BJ had a breath in her lungs, this guy would not get hold of Lyndsey. "My body might be a bit slower since retiring, but my mind's still sharp. And I've got plenty of fight left in me."

"No doubt."

She jumped at the sound of Riley's voice, almost forgetting he was there with her.

"As you can see, there's not a lot." Riley leaned back in his chair. "Just enough to want to keep anyone's child away from the guy."

As much as BJ would rather remain home to finish her thousand-piece puzzle than take a seven-hour drive to Jacksonville, she knew she had no choice. Lyndsey's father had asked for her help, and she'd not let him down.

She straightened her shoulders. Rain pelted against the window overlooking the parking lot. It would be slow travelling in this weather. Good thing she'd gotten up early. She shoved the documents back into the file and grabbed her purse.

"I best be going."

"Be careful." Riley stood up and walked her to his office door.

"I always am."

"Not always." He raised his eyebrows.

"By the way, why are you here so early?" She looked over her shoulder at her nephew. "I can't imagine it's just to give me a file."

"Major car accident near Pike's field. Two kids killed." Sadness filled his eyes. "Appears they crossed the center line and ran into a semi."

"Oh, no."

"Yeah. They were heading to Nashville from the University of Georgia, taking the scenic route."

She patted Riley on his chin. How he dealt with this everyday was beyond her. "Well, tell Calley I'll be back as soon as possible to help her with the babe." She missed living with Riley. But the last thing she wanted was to be in the way of his new family. "Here goes nothing."

After Riley kissed her on the cheek, she ran out to her car to avoid getting soaked. BJ paused after starting the engine, bowed her head and folded her hands. "Lord, please hold on to the family of those children killed. And give me the know-how to keep Lyndsey from this man's grip. Or at least forgive me if I end up shooting this piece of garbage. It'd sure be easier if you just took care of him for me. And please God, don't let Lyndsey end up like Bernadette Lewis."

RONALD "RANSOM" MCNEELY glanced at the four small photographs taped to the dashboard. He smiled. While out shopping one day, Bernadette had insisted they take pictures in one of those boxes in the middle of the mall. Mugging for the camera, doing fish lips, smiling, and her kissing him on the cheek. All a reminder of how much fun it had been getting to know her.

His smile vanished in an instant.

She had been too young to die, especially the way she did. How could someone toss her along the side of the road like a bag of garbage? His jaw tightened.

Someone should pay, and if he had any say, that would be Cliff Mason, for selling her to the guy who killed her. There had to be proof Mason trafficked in children. And once Ransom found it, the pimp would spend his life in a jail cell for what he put countless kids through or better yet, get a needle in his arm.

Not a good Christian thought, but Ransom wasn't exactly God's biggest fan right now. Good thing he still had a bit of concern for the afterlife, or he'd have made sure Mason disappeared like the teenagers he sold. And his death wouldn't be by strangulation like Bernadette's. No, Mason deserved a much slower, more agonizing demise. He warranted all the pain Ransom imagined doling out. Something perfected from his days with the CIA. He shook the thoughts from his head, instead focusing on the job at hand.

Getting Mason arrested and convicted would be all the justice Ransom needed. Once Mason was looking at life in prison, hopefully, he'd lead the authorities to the one responsible for Bernadette's death.

Ransom stomach grumbled for lunch. He circled the Jacksonville Publix grocery store parking lot twice before coming across someone backing from a spot in the third row. Once parked, he twisted in a failed attempt to stretch his back. His body screamed for exercise. Sitting in a car playing detective made it hard on the joints of a man his age. Maybe he should do a quick walk around the strip mall. It might alleviate some of the tension in his muscles. Ransom opened the van's door to the stifling afternoon heat. Too hot to walk anywhere today. How could anyone want to put up with this humidity?

On his way to the store's entrance, he grabbed a cart someone had left on the grass median. A blast of cool air hit him when he walked through the sliding glass doors. It felt good coming in from the ninety-two-degree weather. Unseasonably warm for May.

He walked to the far-right aisle, tossing a loaf of whole wheat bread into the cart, then strolled over and grabbed a jar of peanut butter. At the end of another aisle, he picked up several boxes of beef jerky. Next, produce. Apples, oranges, carrots, and celery were best for a stakeout. He'd have preferred bananas, but they browned too quickly in a warm car.

Reaching for a bag of Red Delicious apples on sale, Ransom stopped short. His heart ratcheted up a notch. On the other side of the produce aisle stood Betty Jo Owens. He swore he'd stepped back in time. She hadn't changed much in the last twenty-five years. Though her hair was now silver instead of blond, her gray eyes still held a hint of mischief even while simply examining a tomato.

Memories of his assignment in South Korea washed over him. Cool nights, great food, and getting to know the female army officer who helped him take down a traitor.

"BJ? Betty Jo, is that you?" He rolled his cart toward her. A glimpse at her left hand still showed a wedding ring. Disappointment smashed his initial excitement.

She did a double take. Her hand went to her chest. "Ransom. Is that you? What are you doing here?"

"Buying my veggies." He grabbed a stalk of celery from a nearby bin. "You look wonderful."

She didn't acknowledge the compliment. Instead, she placed a bag of carrots in the green basket she carried on her arm. "I mean what are you doing in Jacksonville? I can't imagine the CIA has a need for a spy here."

Her words came out curt. Could she still be holding a grudge?

"I'm retired," Ransom said. "Decided to move to the sunshine." He stepped toward her. A subtle hint of vanilla floated his way. Ransom couldn't tell if the aroma came from her perfume or the baked goods in her basket. "How about we do dinner and get caught up? You and your husband, of course."

"Perry died a few years back." Sadness filled her eyes.

"I'm sorry to hear that." And he meant it. He knew how much she'd loved her husband.

"Besides, I'm only here for a couple of days visiting family." Her sadness disappeared quickly, and neutrality took over. She tossed some spinach leaves into her basket. "Take care. It was good to see you again." Her icy stare told him she was anything but glad to see him. She turned on her heel and stalked off. Her purse swung in rhythm with her stride.

He couldn't help but grin recalling that same attitude when he knew her in South Korea. She'd been a spitfire then, and it appeared not much had changed since he'd seen her last. He finally tore his gaze away from her.

It was probably a good thing she didn't want to do dinner since he had more important issues to contend with. And he couldn't afford a distraction like BJ with another girl's life on the line.

BJ IDLED THE JEEP IN the grocery store parking lot. After she'd finished her shopping, she had caught sight of Ransom checking out and actually hid until he left the store. Decades later, and her irritation still lingered. She had to let go of the past.

"Ransom." *Of all the people for You to bring back into my life, Lord.* More likely the devil. Nights filled with laughing and falling in love. Inappropriate feelings and actions for a woman who had a wonderful husband back home. She knew it'd been adultery in her mind.

A fleeting reminder of that first kiss rushed in. She was sure Ransom had garnered his nickname because he could hold any woman hostage with his beautiful blue eyes and sharp wit. A shiver drifted in recalling the cold nights in Seoul. The remembered flavor of the food sold by pojangmacha, the street vendors, crossed her tongue. How she missed the good sashimi. She had yet to find a place that compared to the restaurants in South Korea.

Funny. Since Perry died, she'd never given a second glance to another man. So why did her heart want to burst from her chest with one look at Ransom? His hair, while still dark brown, held bits of gray sprinkled throughout. How could anyone who'd lived the life he had still look so good? And she didn't miss the fact that his T-shirt tightened at his biceps.

She recalled those warm, strong arms holding her. Heat flushed through her body.

She mentally shook her head. All wonderful memories, but they had to be selective recollections because not all could have been good. Especially since Ransom had used her to advance his career and hurt her deeply. If that reminder didn't kill any type of emotion within her, nothing would.

Time to shift her attention back to the reason she'd come to Jacksonville. BJ put the blue Jeep in gear and drove east on Beach Boulevard to Hogan Road. Once off the main street, she took a couple of rights and one left turn. A silver Chevrolet van sat near the corner leading into the cul-de-sac. Dark tinted windows kept her from being able to see inside. BJ swung wide to get around it and drove to the white stucco house. Caladiums aligned the yard, and oval beveled glass decorated the front door. She smiled at how well her nephew was doing.

BJ pulled her vehicle into the driveway behind the black Nissan Pathfinder. After another quick prayer, she shoved Mason's file into one of the grocery bags and marched up the stone walkway.

On the second ring of the bell, Phillip greeted her. Worry lines creased his forehead since the last time she'd seen him. Having teenagers would do that to you. Or so BJ had heard. The closest she had to her own child was Riley, the nephew she'd taken in when her brother-in-law and his wife died in an automobile accident. Riley had wanted to be a police officer from the day he moved in at age eleven and stayed true to that conviction. He'd never given her or Perry any trouble. Again she smiled. Those selective memories.

"Miriam's in the back." Phillip helped her unload the groceries then led her to the screened-in patio. Like his cousin Riley, Phillip wasn't much for words.

His wife rose from her padded chair and hugged BJ. After a few pleasantries, Miriam returned to her seat.

BJ looked up at a military plane from the nearby naval base buzzing across the clear sky. The yard looked postcard perfect, from the crisp blue pool to the two date palms in each corner of the backyard near the red wood fence.

"I can't believe you both think this is such a big deal," Miriam said. "It's just a teen infatuated with an older man."

"She'd been drinking when she came home last Friday." Phillip held his hands on his hips. "Something needs to be done before it's too late."

"She promised she wouldn't do it again. And he'll get tired of her like older boys do." Miriam let out a sigh as if remembering something in her past. "Young girls think it's cool to date a guy that old."

"He's *too* old. Someone in his mid-twenties shouldn't want to hang out with a fourteen- year-old. There's only one reason for it." Phillip winced. "And I'm not about to let that happen. You shouldn't want it either."

Miriam's head titled sideways. She looked like she was about to bite his head off.

"He's more than that," BJ said before their argument could get out of hand. She relayed what she'd discovered regarding Cliff Mason.

Neither parent spoke until she finished. When BJ told them about the missing girl who turned up dead, Phillip's eyes widened, and he started pacing. Miriam's face paled. BJ allowed the information to sink in.

"I sure hope this works," Miriam whispered.

"Where is Lyndsey?" BJ sat back on the thick floral cushion on the loveseat.

"Still in bed." Miriam brushed a strand of hair off her forehead. "It's hard to get her up in the morning on the weekends. Getting her to church is like fighting a wild tiger."

"I don't know what we're going to do with her during summer once school's out." Phillip placed his hands on his hips. "She might be too far gone."

"You are definitely your mother's son," BJ shook her head. "Your momma practically said the same thing when you thought drinking was cool. I just had to show you otherwise." BJ hopped up from her seat. "Now, let's go pull her out of bed. It's time to get the show on the road."

A CAR'S BASS DROWNED out the plane flying overhead. Ransom wiped the back of his neck. Jacksonville humidity was a killer, especially when spending the day sitting in a vehicle. He massaged the tight knot at the back of his neck.

He'd still not gotten his bearings since leaving Publix. Just his luck the Jeep Cherokee with the Georgia license plate in the driveway held BJ. Now she sat inside the house he kept surveillance on. His best chance of getting Cliff Mason lived inside that house. But Ransom would now have to go through BJ to get to Lyndsey Chapel. His grip tightened on the steering wheel. How could he justify his plan to anyone, much less her?

A bead of sweat rolled along Ransom's jawline. If this kept up, the police might find him in a puddle on the floorboard. He started the Chevy and turned the A/C to high.

He rolled the windows down, wishing for air. No such luck.

Two boys strolled past, their pants below their backsides. Ransom let loose a harrumph. Why would anyone want to look so ridiculous? Too many moms these days would rather be friends than a parent, and men would rather be sperm donors than fathers.

Like you. Ransom's heart jolted. The words bounced into his mind before he could stop them. While true, he'd like to think he wasn't the same selfish man from years ago. A friend once told him those insults came from the devil who liked to remind him of his past sins. It kept him from feeling the full forgiveness of God's love. Ransom knew the Lord forgave him for all the fornication of his past. Unfortunately, he couldn't say the same for the daughter who'd grown up without a father.

Ransom startled at the ringing cell phone in the console. He pulled it out and glanced at the caller I.D. Too much to ask that it be Darcy. But an absentee dad shouldn't expect instant love when he bounced into his daughter's life.

"Hello, Frazier," Ransom said. "What can I do for you?"

"Ransom, I won't beat around the bush," his former boss said. "The guy you're sniffing around, Cliff Mason, also has the interest of the DEA. They want you to back off."

"Do they know he sells young kids and is basically responsible for my granddaughter's death?"

"There's no proof."

"Not yet," Ransom snapped. "But we both know if they get him for drugs, he'll make a deal for immunity and not serve a minute in jail."

"I'm just relaying the message. Do with it what you want."

"I suggest you let them know to stay out of my way," Ransom growled. His dealings with the DEA in the past had always left a dent in their sides. "I might have aged a bit since leaving the Agency, but I haven't lost my edge."

"You were good when you retired at fifty-six, but all those years of sitting around can make a difference." Hesitation dripped over the line. After a moment, Frazier added, "And these traffickers don't care who they kill."

"You just let the DEA know to stay out of my way." Ransom hung up, not waiting for a reply. Six years wasn't that long. A man couldn't easily forget what had been drilled into his head every day for thirty years.

The DEA stood low on his list of issues right now. Getting past BJ was first. Little doubt she'd never forgive him for knowingly allowing someone she knew close to a predator.

Of course, if Cliff Mason tangled with BJ that would be good news for Ransom's side. In fact, if she was half the determined woman she'd been all those years ago, Ransom almost felt sorry for Cliff Mason.

Almost.

THIS IS THE END OF Chapter 1 of *One Last Breath*. **To read more, order on Amazon at your favorite book retailer.**

About the Author

KATHRYN J. BAIN'S FIRST release *Breathless* came out January 13, 2012. She has won several awards for her writing including First Place in the International Digital Awards (IDA), First Place in the Royal Palm Literary Awards, Second and Third Place in the Heart of Excellence Readers' Choice Contest, and more.

She became a bestselling author in 2020 when her book *The Chain You Forge* hit number one under Holiday Fiction category and stayed there for four days.

She is the former President of Florida Sisters in Crime and Public Relations Director and Membership Director for Ancient City Romance Authors.

She has been a paralegal for over thirty years and works for an attorney who specializes in elder law.

Kathryn grew up in Coeur d'Alene, Idaho. In 1981, she moved to Boise, but it apparently wasn't far enough south, because two years later she headed Jacksonville, Florida and has lived in the sunshine ever since.

I Need Your Help

1. WRITE A REVIEW. It doesn't have to be elaborate, just something as simple as "I really liked this book."

2. Share my books with your friends and on social media. Word of mouth works better for book sales than any form of advertisement.

3. Post of picture of you reading one of my books and tag me on Facebook or Twitter. (Or your dog, cat, horse, etc.)

4. Join my newsletter for updates. Sign up at https://landing.mailerlite.com/webforms/landing/g4n8h9.

Other Available Titles from Kathryn J. Bain

<u>THE LINCOLNVILLE MYSTERY Series</u>

Breathless, 2012

Catch Your Breath, 2012

One Last Breath, 2014

Take Her Breath Away, 2016

<u>THE KT MORGAN SHORT SUSPENSE SERIES</u>

A Touch of Suspense (Vol. 1-3 of the KT Morgan Short Suspense Series), 2017

A Touch of Suspense (Vol 4-6 of the KT Morgan Short Suspense Series), 2022

The Visitor, pub. 2014

Small Town Terror, 2015

The Reunion, pub. 2016

Run Away, pub. 2019

The Game, pub. 2020

Sucker Punched, 2021

<u>Other FICTION books available</u>

Chasing a Dead Man, 2021

Fade to the Edge, 2019

The Chain You Forge, 2017, #1 Bestseller in Holiday Fiction

<u>MIDDLE-GRADE</u>

Seven Sisters Road, co-written with Jessi Bain, pub. 2020

* 9 7 9 8 2 2 3 5 3 5 0 0 3 *